TWO NIGHTS IN PARIS

DELANEY DIAMOND

GARDEN AVENUE PRESS

Two Nights in Paris by Delaney Diamond

Copyright © 2019, Delaney Diamond

Garden Avenue Press

Atlanta, Georgia

ISBN: 978-1-946302-03-8 (Ebook edition)

ISBN: 978-1-946302-04-5 (Paperback edition)

www.delaneydiamond.com

ree at last!

Stephan Brooks stepped out into the night, relieved to finally be released after spending hours in a holding cell. One of his family's attorney's, Brit Wong, walked ahead of him.

Brit, a slender man with his hair, mustache, and beard peppered with gray, was a partner and founding member of Abraham, MacKenzie & Wong, a mid-sized law firm with offices in Atlanta, Los Angeles, and New York. His firm handled any number of personal issues for Stephan's mother, and she paid a large retainer to have them—but more specifically, Brit—on call for the family, which included cleaning up the messes Stephan got himself into.

On his way to meet friends for dinner, Stephan's red Ferrari had been pulled over for speeding on the highway. Unfortunately, the officer was new on the job and didn't know Stephan came from a wealthy, prominent family. He smelled weed and saw what was left of a blunt in the cupholder and the next thing Stephan knew, he was in the back seat of a patrol car. Luckily, it hadn't taken much for Brit to reach out to the family's friends in law enforcement and ensure he didn't have to spend the night in jail.

Stephan followed the attorney into the back of the waiting limo and met the hard gaze of his mother, Sylvie Johnson.

Crap. He hadn't expected her to be here. He thought he'd be able to go home and have plenty of time to come up with an excuse for what happened.

Diamonds dripped from Sylvie's earlobes, and she wore a long black gown—probably one of her own designs—with white gloves that came up to the elbows. She eyed his attire with tight lips, and he wished he looked better. He'd only been back in the country for a couple of days. He went to a three-day birthday party in the Seychelles but remained for a couple of weeks afterward, soaking up the sun and enjoying life at a slower pace.

He hadn't shaved recently or gotten a haircut, so his normally smooth face had facial hair, and the hair on his head was longer and showed off his natural, loose curls. The worst of his appearance was probably the worn jeans and a black T-shirt emblazoned with the words *Orgasm Donor* on the front.

"Did you have a good time?" Sylvie arched an eyebrow at him.

Stephan braced for the scolding about to come his way. Of course he did not have a good time in jail, but he had to appear adequately contrite to calm his mother's ire and make sure the fallout from his bad decision did not have repercussions for days to come.

"No, I did not. I'm sorry, Mother."

She didn't soften, not even a little bit. "Your father is not pleased, and neither am I. He said I should have left you there to teach you a lesson."

He wasn't surprised his father had made such a suggestion. Oscar Brooks was much stricter than Sylvie when it came to their sons. His father believed she coddled them too much, and in actuality, she did. On the other hand, she felt the need to toughen her daughters. He and his brother had taken full advantage of the special treatment over the years. In his mother's eyes, they did no wrong, and she had gotten them—well, Stephan mostly—out of numerous problems over the years.

He suspected that much of her decisions were because for fifteen years she and his father had been divorced, and his mother felt some guilt over the fact that Oscar lived in a different state and they were not able to have, in her opinion, a proper male influence. As a result, she became too lenient and extra-protective of her sons.

"I'm glad you didn't leave me there," Stephan said.

Sylvie breathed a slow breath. "You must stop this. I need you to do better, Stephan."

She turned away from him to gaze out at the passing buildings, but not before he saw an emotion on her face that she'd never directed at him before. Disappointment.

Pain twisted in his chest and kept him from speaking as the limousine rolled down the street in silence. He didn't know this side of his mother. The woman he grew up with thought her kids were perfect and insisted they did no wrong, even when she knew they had.

He slumped against the leather seat, his gaze landing on Brit, who politely averted his eyes to documents on his lap now that he'd accomplished the task of getting Stephan free.

None of them said a word during the rest of the ride. The limo pulled up outside of the Fox Theatre, where Sylvie had been attending a charity event. Oscar was probably still inside.

Ever since his parents' reconciliation, his mother had been less forgiving of his behavior and less generous with the money she disbursed for his leisurely lifestyle. Much of those changes were because of his father, and resentment settled in Stephan's gut.

Sylvie turned to him. "We need to talk, but not tonight."

"Yes, Mother."

The driver came around and opened the door. Before she exited the vehicle, Sylvie took a good look at her son. "I want you to come to my office on Monday so we can talk in person. I have an appointment at eight, and then another engagement around ten, so I'll squeeze you in at nine o'clock. Be prompt."

"I will be." If she wanted him there at six o'clock in the morning, he'd be there. Right now, he was at her mercy and needed to get back on her good side.

Sylvie walked toward the entrance of the building, and the driver climbed in and took off.

"What do you think, Brit?"

"Do you really want to know my opinion?" the attorney asked.

"I asked, didn't I?"

"If I had to guess, I'd say you used your last life."

Over the years, Brit every so often pointed out that Stephan was using one of his nine lives, his chances, much like a cat did. Stephan laughed every time because he didn't have a worry in the world as he lived the good life that others only fantasized about. Besides, he always sweet-talked his mother and got back on her good side. Obviously, Brit did not believe that was a possibility this time.

"What makes you say that?" Stephan asked.

"I've worked for your mother for a long time. I've seen her get you out of all kinds of scrapes, but I can tell that this time she's had enough."

"But how?" Stephan asked, a little bit of panic bubbling up inside him. He nervously stared at the attorney, waiting anxiously for his reply. As if his answer determined whether or not his relationship with his mother was forever destroyed.

"Because for as long as I've known Sylvie Johnson, whenever you got yourself into trouble, she's been there, right beside you, fighting for you whether you want her to or not. Tonight, she came to make sure that you were okay. But instead of staying with you like she used to, she went back to the event and has effectively sent you home. That's the first time I've ever seen her do that. And that's how I know you've used your last life."

Stephan mulled the attorney's words. His mother certainly didn't seem as worried about him as she'd been in the past. She was annoyed and disappointed.

He dropped his head to the back of the leather seat and closed his eyes. As much as he hated to admit it, he knew the attorney was right.

CHAPTER 2

*O*n Monday morning, Stephan plodded into his mother's
large office, decorated in white—her favorite color—with
splashes of tan and pale rose. Sheer drapes covered windows at
her back and allowed sunlight to come in and brighten the room.

He dropped into the chair before her glass desk. He'd shaved,
cut his hair, and made sure to dress more appropriately today in a
long-sleeved shirt and chinos.

Sylvie was on the phone and held up one finger while continuing her conversation in Spanish, a language which he also spoke
fluently.

He couldn't help but admire his mother. She'd bucked tradition
and instead of setting up shop in New York or California like most
designers, chose Atlanta, Georgia. She was a successful businesswoman, albeit one who started her career with millions of dollars
in her pocket, but had turned that money into a multibillion-dollar
enterprise called SJ Brands. Her fashion, makeup, and furniture
lines were also under the SJ Brands name, while SJ Media was the
name for her company that produced films and funded documen-
taries. She was doing what she loved instead of working in the
family's beer and restaurant businesses, but she'd had every right
to inherit a portion of the conglomerate. Furthermore, she weath-

ered the storm of a divorce and taking care of four children, somehow managing to keep her sanity while she grew her companies.

He hated to disappoint her and had considered lying and blaming the weed on one of his friends, but that was the coward's way out. He was more than ready to make up for what he'd done. Hopefully, she'd see his contrition and cut him a break.

Sylvie hung up the phone and stared across the desk at him.

Stephan grinned at her, hoping to warm the icy freeze in the room. "You look great today."

She wore her hair down in a spool of black silk that tumbled down her back, a hairstyle she wore more frequently ever since she and his father got back together.

"I look great every day."

He lost his smile. This conversation was going to be harder than anticipated. He decided to meet the problem head-on. "I know I screwed up big time, and I want you to know that I'm really sorry. I'm going to do better. Moving forward, you're going to see a whole new Stephan."

Sylvie folded her hands on the desk and looked steadily at him. "You're saying everything I want you to say. Like you always have."

Damn. She really was pissed.

"I mean it this time."

His mother sighed heavily. "From the beginning, you've always given me so much trouble. You were my most difficult pregnancy."

Here we go, Stephan thought, fighting with everything in him not to roll his eyes.

"You were born late. Simply *refused* to be born and were seven days overdue. Then I went into labor, and oh my goodness." She shook her head.

Twenty hours of labor.

"Twenty hours of labor, Stephan! You've never been easy, and you grew more difficult as you got older. I didn't help matters by letting you get away with murder, bailing you out every time you got into trouble, and in general not giving you the tools you need to become a successful and properly functioning adult. All of that changes today."

She said the last in a steely voice that made Stephan pay attention.

"You need to find a job. I'm canceling your credit cards and cutting your allowance."

Stephan went rigid with shock. "What! You can't do that!"

"I'm afraid I can, darling. The changes won't be immediate. You have thirty days to find work. After the thirty days are up, you will be responsible for most of your expenses." She sat back in the chair.

"By how much are you cutting my allowance?"

"Fifty percent."

"Fifty percent! I'll starve!" Had what he'd done really warranted such a harsh punishment? "Did Father put you up to this?" He was pretty sure his father put this idea into her head.

"I do have a mind of my own, Stephan," Sylvie said dryly. She stood and came to stand beside the chair, resting her bottom on the edge of her desk. "You will not starve. You'll be fine. You have to learn to budget and earn your own money to spend."

Stephan inwardly seethed. "I don't understand why you're doing this."

"It's for your own good. You have to learn to be responsible, and I feel as if it's my fault that you haven't been responsible all these years."

"I am responsible. I've learned my lesson, I promise."

"Not from what I've seen."

"What kind of work could I possibly do?" All he knew was how to spend money, give orgasms, and have a good time. He had virtually no work experience and wasn't capable of anything else.

Sylvie shrugged. "Perhaps you could work at a coffee shop."

"Very funny." There was no way the money he earned working

at a coffee shop would offset the loss in income from his decreased allowance and canceled credit cards.

"Well, I'm certainly not going to refer you to any of my friends, and you can't work for your cousins at Johnson Enterprises."

Johnson Enterprises was the umbrella organization that made up the multi-billion-dollar beer and restaurant empire on his mother's side of the family. At the moment, his cousins owned and ran Johnson Brewing Company, the number-one beer company in the country.

"Why not?"

"As far as my friends, my reputation would be at stake. I'm not taking any chances with you embarrassing me. You have embarrassed me enough, and believe me, I am not happy about this weekend's events. Then, of course, there's the situation of the summer you spent in Seattle working at Johnson Enterprises headquarters. Need I remind you what happened?"

Stephan winced. "No."

He'd majorly screwed up. Since he was family, he didn't think he had to work as hard as the other employees. He came in late, left early, and didn't turn in assignments on time. His cousin Cyrus, the company's no-nonsense CEO, eventually fired him. Not his finest moment at all.

"Of course, you could always work here," Sylvie said. "Ella and Reese have positions in my company, so I'm inviting you to work here as well."

His older sister Ella was the vice president of operations, overseeing all their mother's businesses, and his younger brother Reese worked in the IT department, no doubt being groomed to take over after the current CIO left.

"Work here under your thumb?" Stephan grumbled. Sylvie arched an eyebrow at him. "I didn't mean that."

"I'm sure you didn't. Because you know better."

"I can't work here, Mother. What will I do? Sew dresses?"

"Don't be nasty, darling, it's unbecoming. I'll find a spot for you if you tell me what you're interested in. You can work in any of my companies or all of them. It's completely up to you, but you have to make a decision."

"And what if I don't want to work for you?"

"Then you can go work at a coffee shop," Sylvie said with a tight smile.

Stephan smelled a setup. While it was true that he'd made a mistake over the weekend, it was not his first brush with the law. In the past, he'd been caught driving on a suspended license and been in a couple of physical altercations, among other things. He understood if his mother was getting tired of cleaning up his messes, but he sensed there was more amiss. It would be impossible for him to find a job that made up the loss in income from his cut allowance, and to do so within the timeframe she stipulated.

I could always deejay, he thought. But that didn't appeal to him as much as it should. Being a celebrity DJ used to be fun and paid well, but it was still work—late night work that he preferred to do only on an occasional basis, more as a hobby. If it became his full-time job, he'd hate it.

The only way to meet all the requirements was to work for Sylvie, which he was starting to suspect was the endgame anyway. Sylvie was expected to transition the conglomerate to her children eventually, but with his track record, he'd never considered she'd want him to be one of those children. If he came on board now, if he showed her he was no good at his job, maybe she'd leave him alone once and for all, and then he'd only have a short wait until he received a huge chunk of his inheritance after he turned thirty.

Still…

"I don't have any skills," Stephan said.

"You speak several languages fluently, and you worked for your father one summer."

Oscar brokered boat sales, and that's how he met Sylvie.

"That was ages ago. I was a kid, and selling boats is not the same as selling furniture or clothing or working in the film industry."

"No, but the same skill sets apply. You're a people person and can use that to your advantage. I think you'd be a star in business development, working with the SJ Brand stores and the third-party stores that carry my brand."

Stephan deflated. She had an answer for every objection.

Her gaze softened a fraction. "You know this is for the best. You're twenty-nine years old, and it's time for you to grow up. At least try. For me, hmm? If you don't like working in business development, we'll see if you fit in somewhere else."

"All right," Stephan muttered.

Sylvie's face brightened. "Good."

A knock sounded at the door.

"Come in," she called.

Stephan heard the door open.

"I'm sorry! I didn't know you were in a meeting. Inez wasn't at her desk."

With his back turned, he couldn't see the person who spoke, but immediately his ears perked up at the soft, alluring sound of her voice. A voice he'd heard before.

"It's fine. Come in."

Sylvie waved the woman forward, and Stephan twisted in the chair enough to catch sight of her as she approached.

Roselle Parker was a mildly attractive woman holding two sketchpads at her side. She had cinnamon-brown skin, and her shoulder-length hair was styled into bouncy curls.

Sylvie took a couple of steps toward the younger woman. "Stephan, have you met Roselle before? She's one of my fashion directors, overseeing accessories and the women's workwear lines. She is one of my best employees. Whatever I toss at her, she handles. I don't know what I'd do without her."

"Thank you." Roselle blushed and lowered her gaze in a bashful manner.

"Stephan is going to start working here very soon, in business development. I don't believe you've met before, have you?"

"Not formally. I've seen him once or twice in the building, and once briefly in the break room," Roselle replied with a smile.

11

A nice smile to hide the fact that she'd been rude to him in that same break room.

Stephan came to his feet. "Nice to see you again."

He towered over her, so she had to look up at him with a pair of bottomless dark brown eyes that sucked him in with their radiance. Like he did with every woman, he assessed her fuckability.

She gave him a firm handshake with very soft hands that sent an unexpected surge through him. His fingers tightened around hers, and he examined her features as if he had to sketch them later for an art final. She was cute, with prominent cheekbones and full, inviting-looking lips. A bit on the slender side, though not too skinny for him. Under her silk blouse, her breasts were too small for a handful but still a decent size. She had a small waist hidden beneath slimming black slacks, and dark heels gave her a little height.

Final assessment, he'd definitely do her. He wanted to do her if only she'd give him a shot.

Roselle abruptly withdrew her hand, cutting off contact and leaving Stephan feeling oddly bereft of her touch.

"I brought those sketches you asked for," she said, returning her attention to Sylvie in a way that made him feel as if she were purposely ignoring him.

"Good. Let's see what you have."

Stephan reclaimed his seat, and both women rounded the desk. Sylvie sat down and put on her black-framed glasses, while Roselle showed her the designs.

Sylvie flipped through the pages. "Oh, these are lovely. I like this one a lot." She tapped the page with a forefinger.

"I do, too. I think that skirt works for next year's spring line."

"Oh, absolutely. But instead of this blue, I'd go deeper to indigo."

"Yes, I see what you mean."

As Roselle bent over the desk, she tucked strands of hair behind her ear and laughed quietly with his mother as she pointed to something on a sheet of paper. She was definitely hot.

"That's fascinating. We must do that," Sylvie said. She made a check mark in the top right corner of one of the sheets.

"I thought you would agree."

Was Roselle really that amenable or was she one of those people who kissed Sylvie's butt because they were terrified of her?

Sylvie flipped to another page. "How are your plans going for the trip to Paris?" she asked.

Roselle straightened. "I re-confirmed the meetings this morning."

"Wonderful. I hope you've scheduled some free time, too."

"You're going to love Paris," Stephan said.

"I'd like to stay an extra day if it's okay with you." Roselle spoke directly to his mother as if he hadn't spoken.

Was she ignoring him, or was that his imagination? He wasn't used to being ignored, especially not by women.

Sylvie removed her glasses and set them on the desk. "Of course. One cannot go to Paris without doing a little sightseeing. And you've never been before, have you?"

"No, never. I've never been out of the country. I had to get a passport for this trip." Roselle gave a little laugh.

"Then, by all means, take an extra day to do a tour. Visit the Louvre or take a trip on one of the boats that cruise down the Seine River. Enjoy yourself."

"Thank you!" Roselle's eyes lit up with excitement, and Stephan couldn't help but stare.

Sylvie looked at him. "Roselle is meeting with the representatives of a high-end department store in Paris, Rue de la Mode. Our lines do very well at other Parisian retailers, and they want to partner with us to release a line exclusive to their stores—clothes, shoes, accessories, and bed linens."

"You've never done bed linens before," Stephan said. He didn't know much about his mother's business, but he did know that.

"No, I haven't, but I'm open to the idea. The company is interested in a long-term relationship. Roselle is going over there to meet with them and check out their stores."

"To see if they're worthy of carrying your brand?" Stephan asked with mild amusement.

"Exactly. Not everyone is worthy," Sylvie said with a heavy dose of arrogance. "There will be more negotiations afterward, but we want to at least meet with them and start a conversation." She handed the pads to Roselle. "I like what I see with those sketches. Tell them to carry on. Have the rest of them to me by next week."

"I will." Roselle's grin rivaled the sunlight pouring through the windows at Sylvie's back.

She left the room.

"Where were we?" Sylvie asked.

"We were talking about me coming to work for you in business development."

"Oh, yes. So—"

"Can't wait."

"You can't?"

"Yes." Stephan stood. "When do you want me to start?"

CHAPTER 3

*S*ylvie stared at Stephan for a moment, and he looked right back at her. Finally, she stood and came around the desk, hands on her hips. She was shorter than him but intimidating as hell with that stern frown on her face. If he shifted even a little, she'd read his mind and know his thoughts were less then wholesome about her employee.

"What are you up to?"

Stephan laughed. "Isn't this what you wanted? You want me to be responsible and offered me a position with your company. Is that no longer the case?"

He thought again about Roselle. Her smile, the way her eyes lit up when she talked about Paris, and of course that voice—alluring, sweet. He'd already imagined how she'd sound in his bed as he used his skills in all the ways he knew how to give her pleasure. Was she a screamer or a moaner? She had a quiet air about her, so he suspected she was a moaner. But he'd do his best to make her scream.

"Very well, I have every confidence in you. Do not disappoint me, Stephan. Consider this your last chance to impress me. Do I make myself clear?"

"Crystal clear."

"Wonderful." The phone on Sylvie's desk rang, and when she read the caller ID, she smiled and picked up the receiver. "Hello," she purred.

That must be his father on the line.

Sylvie glanced at her watch. "You're early, but that's fine. I'm wrapping up my conversation with Stephan now, and I have wonderful news. He's coming to work for me." She fell silent as she listened to his father talk. Then she nodded. "Of course, darling, I know. But I believe he's serious, and I've impressed upon him how serious I am." She locked eyes with Stephan. "Yes, I'll be right down. I will. See you in a few minutes." She hung up the phone. "Your father says hi."

"Tell him I said hi back. Father is your ten o'clock appointment?"

She picked up her purse and tucked it under her arm. "Yes. Your father and I sometimes meet for mid-morning coffee or for lunch. Or we meet in the afternoon for tea. It's not very often, but it was his idea, and I like it. I spend so much time working, and he thought meeting up every so often during the day for thirty minutes or so was a way to keep things fresh between us. He's also insisted we do date nights, where he plans *everything*. It's quite nice."

She was positively glowing, and though he resented his father's influence on her, their reconciliation made her happy.

Sylvie tucked her arm in his, and they walked to the door. "You'll need to go down to HR and fill out the proper paperwork."

Stephan cleared his throat. "In terms of salary, how much are we talking?"

"Enough to get you close to your suspended allowance," Sylvie answered.

Yes! Stephan shouted internally, but kept his expression neutral, nodding with a grave expression on his face. That wasn't perfect, but certainly better than the struggle he'd anticipated.

"You can start tomorrow, arrive at eight o'clock. Touch base with your sister first so she can talk to HR on your behalf and give you an idea of how the company runs. Since she's over operations, I'll let her take over from here."

They walked out of her office, which led directly into an open reception area where Inez's desk was set up. After a brief goodbye to her admin, they stopped at the elevator.

"Remember what I told you." Sylvie tapped her cheek, and Stephan dutifully kissed it.

"I haven't forgotten. Don't worry, I'll be on my best behavior. I won't let you down." He tucked his hands into his pants pockets.

"I certainly hope you don't."

Sylvie entered the elevator cabin. Her disapproving stare was the last thing he saw before the doors closed.

* * *

MINUTES AFTER LEAVING Sylvie's office on shaky legs, Roselle still hadn't recovered from seeing Stephan Brooks again. She stepped into her cluttered office and leaned back against the closed door.

She'd had to tug her hand away from his because...*wow*. Like the first time she'd been in close contact with him, he smelled divine. The fragrance was leather mixed with a hint of citrus. And his voice, low and smooth, brought sex to mind and made her so uneasy she refused to look at him the rest of the time in the meeting because she didn't want him to guess her lustful thoughts.

The first time she'd seen him, she'd only caught the back of his head when he was leaving for lunch with his mother and siblings —something they did once a month. But even the back view had been enough to make an impression on her. There was something about his walk—his *presence*—that impacted her during those brief seconds.

The next time they saw each other, she'd exited the building as he pulled up to the curb to pick up his younger brother, Reese, who stood on the sidewalk chatting with another employee. Most days she took public transportation to work, so she was on her way to the bus stop, but her eyes had remained on him as he rolled down the window and yelled for Reese to hurry up. Then their gazes connected, and the right corner of his lips quirked up knowingly. As if he were used to women staring at him. Right away, she realized she was standing in the middle of the sidewalk, mesmerized like a fool.

With burning cheeks, she rushed away, mortified and praying she'd never see him again. Of course, luck was not with her. They saw each other yet again, this time in the break room. She was on the executive floor for a meeting and had slipped in there for coffee and one of the espresso chocolate-filled beignets a kind employee had brought from a local bakery.

Stephan was also there, punching a Coke from the vending machine. She would have darted out right away, but he saw her, so she mumbled a greeting. He said something about the beignets and pointed out there was only one left.

With a quickness that surprised even her, Roselle snatched up the beignet and slid her tongue along the length of it. "Sorry. I licked it, so now it's mine."

She experienced a sense of satisfaction as Stephan gaped at her. That teasing half-smile that tilted up the right corner of his mouth, as if he was secretly laughing at everyone and everything around him, was completely gone. While he stood there stunned, Roselle poured a cup of coffee.

She had no idea what possessed her to do such a thing. Perhaps to prove to herself that her attraction for him was not real, and perhaps to deflate his ego a little. If he'd thought she was interested in him before that moment, licking the last beignet so he couldn't have it was a great way to squash that theory.

Roselle picked up the beignet with a napkin and headed to the door.

"You know what?"

Stephan's voice stopped her. She should have kept moving but was curious about what he had to say.

"I haven't decided if that was a turn-off or a turn-on. I'm leaning toward the latter."

She'd rushed out, his soft chuckle echoing in her eardrums, intoxicating and devilishly warm in a way that annoyed her.

Today she'd struggled not to stare at him. He had a smooth face, and the hair on his head was cut so low it looked almost straight. Tall and broad, he'd dominated Sylvie's large office, but not in an intimidating way. Everything else in the room receded like the blurred background in a photo, while he remained crisp and sharp and bright in tan chinos and a white, long-sleeved shirt.

He was painfully good-looking, with thick lashes above eyes the same light-brown—whiskey-colored—as his mother's. But where Sylvie's were sharp and assessing, his were filled with a hint of amused interest. He had a thin upper lip, but a full lower one that looked invitingly soft. The kind of lips that were perfect for sucking or nibbling on with her teeth. She'd met his father once when he visited the office, and Stephan had inherited his sandy-gold complexion. Based on the rumors she'd heard, much of his charm, as well.

Roselle shook her head to shake out of her momentary trance. She had a million tasks to complete, and none of them involved mooning over her boss's son like some lovesick preteen with a boy band crush.

In the rectangular-shaped office, her desk sat to the left against a red wall. The desk was almost completely covered with magazines, books, fabric, and patterns. A credenza next to it held her laptop and phone. In the middle of the tiled floor, a long table contained a sewing machine at one end, while textiles, scissors, measuring tape, needles, and other tools of the trade littered its surface. The walls were filled with pictures she'd torn out of magazines, as well as other visuals she'd grouped together in an effort to predict trends and create unified looks for the lines she oversaw.

Her two bookcases were laughably overstuffed, filled with more magazines and fashion books she used as reference materials.

Roselle stepped over a pile of magazines and dropped the sketch pads to the desk. She sat down in her burgundy leather chair. Though she needed to get work done, her mind wandered again to Stephan.

Did he have an Instagram account? She didn't, but everyone else did nowadays.

With curiosity getting the better of her, she set her laptop on the desk, logged in, and did a quick search. She found his handle and began scrolling.

If the pictures on his page were any indication, she and he were complete opposites. He was flamboyant and threw raunchy parties that celebrities and socialites were invited to. She, on the other hand, was a loner. Her roommate was a traveling nurse, gone all week for work and on the weekends because of an active social life. Roselle spent her nights and weekends sewing or poring over fashion magazines. When she wasn't doing that, she ate Chinese food out of a container and watched movies on Netflix.

Stephan also naturally had the kind of confidence she had to fake. There were plenty of pictures of him with his head held at an arrogant angle, arm casually thrown around some young woman's neck who was either kissing his jaw or her body was turned toward him while she stared into the camera.

Roselle should be turned off, not turned on by the arrogance that practically oozed from his pores. He was obviously a cocky pretty boy who'd had everything handed to him his entire life, and whose sense of entitlement must be one hundred miles wide because of his wealth. He was definitely not her type.

She paused on a photo of Stephan seated on a sofa with a scantily-clad young actress on his lap. Two beautiful people stared into the camera.

Roselle laughed out loud. "Roselle, you're not his type, either," she murmured.

She'd have to keep her distance until this silly crush—or whatever it was—went away. With Stephan working in business development, located on the same floor as her office, they'd run into each other from time to time, but she'd be sure to avoid him whenever possible.

"Get back to work," she admonished herself. She exited Instagram.

Pushing thoughts of Stephan from her mind, she picked up the phone to call a vendor.

CHAPTER 4

*R*oselle walked briskly from her office through the quiet reception area, on her way to a late lunch. She was starving.

One of the admins wore headphones over her ears as she transcribed dictation, and the other admin waved while talking on the phone. Roselle waved back. The two women provided support to Roselle, the other fashion directors, and the creative director of the furniture line.

Her mind was going a thousand miles a minute, excitement practically thrumming through her veins. After talking to her aunt last night, she'd stayed up late scouring the Internet for details about Paris and had bookmarked dozens of tourist sites.

She found details about the riverboats that cruised the Seine that Sylvie had mentioned. They were called Bateaux Mouches, and if there was time, she definitely wanted to take one of those excursions. But there were two things she was absolutely determined to do—stroll down the Champs-Élysées and take a selfie with the Eiffel Tower in the background.

To think, three years ago she'd been in a bad place after...*no*. She'd promised herself she wouldn't go there.

Roselle went down the hall and came to a full stop when she

saw Stephan in front of the elevator. She hadn't seen him in a couple of days. She last saw him on Tuesday, cursing at the copy machine until she showed him how to restart it. Then she'd ducked out and gone back to her office, waiting until she was sure he was gone, before returning to make copies.

Stephan turned in her direction, looking handsome in a dark blue blazer and pale yellow shirt underneath. No tie.

"Hi," she said and then mentally berated herself for the breathless sound of her voice. Why did he make her so nervous?

"Haven't seen you in a couple of days." He flashed a grin, making her belly do a strange little somersault in a blatant display of nerves.

"I've been busy." She came closer but remained a respectful distance from him.

"Going out for a late lunch like me?" he asked.

"Yes," she replied, staring at the closed doors.

"You know what, I kind of get the impression that you don't like me."

She looked at him. "What makes you say that?"

"You hardly ever speak, and when you do, it's in short sentences, as if you can't wait for our conversation to be over."

Roselle had been dodging him but hadn't expected him to call her out. "That's your imagination," she said, returning her gaze to the elevator doors.

"Uh-huh. Where are you going to eat? I'm headed over to Kayak."

Kayak was an upscale restaurant tucked away behind one of the city's most exclusive neighborhoods. She'd never eaten there, but she did know that there was no way he could drive to Kayak, eat lunch, and return to the office within an hour. He was looking at a minimum of two hours. He would probably get away with it, though. One of the privileges of being the owner's son.

"I'm walking to Subway down the street," she replied.

"I've never eaten there. I heard they have good sandwiches. I'll have to try it sometime."

Roselle eyed him skeptically, and he raised an eyebrow at her.

"What's that look for? I'll eat at Subway."

"I doubt that, but okay."

"You don't think I'll do it."

"I'm sure you will," Roselle said, voice laced with a heavy dose of skepticism.

"I'm canceling my car and going to Subway." Stephan removed his phone from his pocket.

"Don't do that on my account."

The elevator doors opened, and they both stepped in. The same way he dominated his mother's office, he filled the car with his presence. From the corner of her eye, she saw his thumbs move quickly over the phone's screen.

"You challenged me, so I'm going to meet that challenge. Hopefully, you don't mind having company." He looked up at her inquiringly.

Roselle shrugged. "I don't mind," she said casually, the thrumming excitement she'd felt a few minutes ago about Paris returned twofold at the thought of lunch with him.

"Good. Then it's settled." He tucked the phone into a pocket.

They nodded at other employees who entered on one of the lower floors, and they all rode the elevator to the lobby. Soon, they were out the door and headed on foot to Subway.

"So, what do you recommend I try at this place?" Stephan asked.

"Any of their sandwiches are good, but I'm partial to the meatball sandwich," Roselle said.

They strolled at a leisurely pace, sticking close enough to talk, but not close enough to touch. When they arrived at Subway, Stephan opened the door and let her enter first. There was a line, and she heard him groan behind her.

"It won't take long," Roselle assured him.

Stephan leaned close to her ear. "How does this work?" he asked, his breath tickling her ear.

She swallowed and turned a little toward him to reply. Their eyes locked for a second before she glanced away. "First, you tell them the bread you want. The choices are there." She pointed at the menu board. "Then you tell them if you want a six-inch or a foot-long."

"Whoa, a six-inch or a foot-long? What kind of establishment is this?" Stephan whispered.

Roselle giggled. "That's the size of your sandwich. Six inches or twelve inches."

"Okay, got you." Amusement filled his light brown eyes.

Roselle continued explaining the process for getting his food. When it was their turn, she placed her order for a six-inch meatball, and Stephan placed his for a foot-long BMT.

They eased down to the register. "I'll pay for both of these sandwiches," Stephan said.

"I can pay for my own meal," Roselle said.

"I'm sure you can, but I want to." He pulled out a credit card and spoke to the clerk. "Make both of them combos and add three of those chocolate chip cookies."

"Thank you," Roselle mumbled.

"Not a problem."

The woman rang up the order, and after they collected drinks and chips, they sat at a table against the wall that two construction workers vacated seconds before.

"So, what does a fashion director do?" Stephan asked, opening the paper wrapped around his sandwich.

"A little bit of everything," Roselle answered, which was one of the many reasons she loved her job. "I have to understand fashion trends and know fashion history and coordinate events. I handle the branding for the two lines I oversee, and I sometimes have to travel. In the past, it's solely been in the United States, but Miss Sylvie wants me to do more international travel." She used to call her Ms. Johnson, but Sylvie had given her permission to call her Sylvie. She'd compromised and called her Miss Sylvie.

"Sounds like you like it."

"I love it. How do you like working in business development so far?" Roselle asked.

"So far, it's not bad, but it's early yet. I look forward to working with you, though," Stephan said.

"We won't be working together," she said, confused. Not unless they were specifically assigned to work together, and she couldn't see that happening.

"You're wrong. You and I are going to become real close." He took a big bite of his sandwich.

"Why do you say that?"

He shrugged. "I have a sixth sense about these things."

"When you say real close—"

"I mean real close." His unwavering gaze met hers.

Oh. "I thought we were just doing lunch."

"We are."

"That didn't sound like lunch conversation. Sounds like you were hitting on me."

"And if I was?"

She paused. "Don't you prefer women who are a little more... glamorous? Actresses, models, that kind of thing?"

He set down his sandwich and finished chewing. "You ever consider modeling yourself?"

"*Me*? No." Roselle shook her head at such a ridiculous suggestion.

"Why not? You have the look."

"No, I don't." She laughed at him.

"Sure. Pretty, great body..." He dropped that gem into the conversation like it was nothing.

Heat crawled up Roselle's neck to her face. "I'm too short for runway."

"You could do print ads. How tall are you? You look about five-four."

"I'm five-five, thank you very much."

"Gotta get that extra inch in there, huh?" he said with a chuckle.

"If I left off an inch on your penis length, you'd insist I add it, wouldn't you?"

His eyebrows flew higher. "Ouch."

"Am I wrong?"

"No, but I didn't expect that from you. You got a little fire in you, Roselle."

He looked at her with renewed interest, but she pretended not to notice, taking a sip of her drink instead.

People always acted surprised whenever she stood up for herself, but she'd learned to do that over the years, though it didn't come naturally. As a quiet personality, she would rather not bring attention to herself, but by perfecting the tough-girl act, she'd created a persona that others related to.

"Now you know," she said.

"Yeah, now I know," Stephan said slowly.

They ate in silence for a few minutes.

"I used to model," Stephan said.

"When?" She shouldn't be surprised. He was tall and had the right look, including great facial bone structure.

"Years ago, when I was fifteen. I started modeling for one of my mother's designer friends and lasted about six months before I quit."

"Why did you quit?"

"Got bored." He wasn't looking at her anymore, and she suspected there was more.

"You quit because of boredom? That doesn't sound like the whole story."

"It's not the whole story."

For a moment, his mask dropped. A frown creased his brow, and she had the surprising urge to smooth it away with her fingers.

He continued. "Having all those people fawning all over me all the time made me uncomfortable. All they ever talked about was my looks, as if.. I don't know, as if there was nothing else there. As if I had no substance, so I quit."

"That sucks when people think of you in a one-dimensional way," Roselle said gently. "Does it still bother you when people fawn all over you?"

The sexy half-smile reemerged. "Nah. Now I use it to my advantage."

The way he looked at her, she might be his next victim.

Stephan shoved the last cookie over to her side of the table. "You can have it."

"Why?"

"Because you moaned a little bit when you ate the last one."

Her cheeks flamed. "Did I?"

He nodded. "I shouldn't have given it to you. Should have licked it and made it mine."

Roselle shifted in her seat. "About that beignet—"

"Don't worry about it. I thought it was funny." Amusement filled his eyes.

"In my defense, I like anything with chocolate. There's another sandwich shop near the office, and they have these chocolate cookies with chocolate chunks, chocolate chips, and M&Ms. They're so good. Thanks for the cookie, by the way." She broke off a piece and popped it in her mouth.

"So, you're a chocoholic. Next time we'll have to stop in there."

"The sandwiches are awful."

"Then we'll only eat the cookies."

Roselle gulped. Why did that sound dirty? Maybe because he'd lowered his voice and his intense gaze suggested he wanted to eat *her*.

"We'll see," she said, a little breathless.

CHAPTER 5

*D*arn it. She was going to be late getting back to the office. Roselle all but ran down the sidewalk.

She didn't punch a clock but was not the type to take advantage and return to work whenever she felt like it. She'd been so busy enjoying Stephan's company she lost track of time. Aside from the flirtatious conversation, he wasn't as bad as she thought.

He wasn't only sexy. He was funny and easy to talk to. The kind of man who made you laugh out loud in public and screwed the hell out of you in private. Though she had no business thinking about him in private.

"You don't have to rush back," Stephan said, taking long, effortless strides and keeping up with ease.

"*You* don't have to rush back," Roselle said pointedly.

She pushed open the glass doors before he had a chance to open them for her.

"Hold the elevator!" she yelled, scurrying across the marble floor to the closing doors.

One of the passengers held them open, and she squeezed in, slightly winded from her accelerated pace. Stephan slid between the doors and stood on the opposite end.

On the third floor, three occupants left. After the sixth floor, they were alone again.

"You're not going to get fired, and if you get into trouble, I'll gladly admit that I'm the reason you were late."

"Thanks, but I'd rather not be late," Roselle said. She stared at the numbers as the cabin climbed higher.

The elevator stopped on their floor and opened to a plain white wall with the words SJ Brands emblazoned on them in gold. There was no reception area. To the left was a set of sofas and the beginning of the creatives department. To the right, another grouping of chairs, and the beginning of the business development department.

Roselle hopped off the elevator.

"Wait a minute," Stephan said, grabbing her upper arm.

His touch sent a flare of heat blazing across her skin and scattered her thoughts. She jerked away, staring at him in shock.

He stepped back and held up his hand. "Sorry."

"No, it's okay. I...it's fine." She rubbed the spot he'd touched. It felt warm as if he were still touching her. She'd feel his touch long after they walked away from each other.

"I know you have to get back to work, but I wanted to see if you'd like to have lunch again sometime."

"Um, maybe."

He frowned. "You didn't enjoy my company?"

"I did, but I usually eat alone."

"Is that what you prefer?"

"Sometimes. It gives me time to think. It's nothing personal."

"Just so you know, I enjoyed your company, even if you didn't enjoy mine."

"I did enjoy your company, but I want to make sure you don't expect more from me. We're coworkers."

He angled his head to the side. "Are you implying I might want more than friendship?"

Wait a minute, hadn't he flirted with her back at Subway? Was she misreading the signals? "I-I didn't mean—"

"I get it, it's hard to resist me."

Roselle opened her mouth to refute the claim, but he interrupted. "Believe me, I know. It's a burden I've carried all my life. I'm aware of the effect I have on women, but there's nothing I can do about these good looks. Blame my parents. I do try my best to tone down the charm. After all, with great power comes great responsibility," he said gravely.

"I'm not sure what to say to such a blatant display of narcissism."

"You could agree to show me the ropes and help me be successful."

"Your mother runs the company, and your sister is second in command," she said pointedly.

"All the more reason why I need help. I have to work hard to impress them. Come on, help a brother out. I'm looking for a friend, someone who can help me understand the fashion industry. If you can't handle being friends with a stunningly attractive man without wanting to jump his bones, then you, madam, have a problem. And you know what, now I don't want to be your friend."

He was using reverse psychology. She knew it, and he probably knew she knew it, and still, the words coming out of her mouth were, "If you're that insistent that you need a friend, I guess we can be friends."

"I don't want you to make an exception for me. I know I'm a newbie in the industry, and you're a seasoned vet."

"I will lower my standards to make an exception for you."

He clutched his chest. "Thank you. I'm speechless with gratitude, milady." He did a little bow.

Roselle laughed. He was too much. No wonder he always had women clinging to him in his Instagram pictures. Who could blame them?

The humor disappeared from Stephan's face, and he leveled that unwavering gaze of his at her again. "But seriously, I had a good time."

Roselle shifted from one foot to another. She needed to get back to work but didn't want to walk away. "I did, too. Thanks for paying for my meal."

"You said that already."

"Thank you again."

"And us eating together won't be a problem, right? No one's going to run up on me in a dark alley?"

"Why would you be in a dark alley?"

"I have no idea."

They both laughed.

"No one will run up on you in a dark alley," Roselle confirmed.

"Good," Stephan said decisively.

Their eyes locked for a moment where time stood still. Then a slow smile came across his lips, and she wondered if he knew her thoughts. Had he guessed how attracted she was to him and how hard she was fighting that attraction?

Even the way he ate was sexy. He ate slowly, chewing each bite as if he were taking his time and savoring every morsel. And when he spoke, the low rumble of his voice made her want to lean in closer. From the time she sat down across from him at lunch, heat settled in her midsection and didn't move. It remained there throughout the entire meal while they talked and laughed, and he flirted.

"See you later, friend." His voice had dipped lower.

"Later." Roselle walked away, wondering if she'd made a mistake agreeing to have lunch with him again.

She had to be careful. Stephan was smooth and charming, and that was a problem. He was like a spider, and before long she might get caught in his web, hopelessly entangled. She shuddered at the thought of what he'd do to her when that happened.

She looked back. He was still standing there. Watching her.

His eyes traveled slowly down her body and left her skin tingling all over. "Enjoy the rest of your day."

"You, too," Roselle said, voice barely audible.

She turned right and hurried through the reception area.

That last look he sent in her direction was not filled with lazy amusement. The heat in his eyes said it all.

He was imagining her naked.

CHAPTER 6

*S*trolling through the open door of his sister Ella's office, Stephan placed a spoonful of the yogurt parfait he was eating as an afternoon snack into his mouth.

He hadn't been able to stop thinking about Roselle since they had lunch together the week before. He was inexplicably drawn to her but was unable to articulate exactly why. He only knew he had to have her, and after that lunch, he wanted her even more.

Ella stood behind her desk, looking like a younger version of their mother in a sharp royal blue pantsuit, hair pinned back in a bun, and her dark skin perfectly made up. She looked confident and self-assured, having come a long way since divorcing that loser none of the family thought was good enough for her.

With one hand on her hip, she looked over the shoulder of their younger brother Reese, who was working on her laptop.

Like him, Reese had inherited their father's complexion but was leaner than Stephan.

"Are you sure you can fix it?" Ella asked in an impatient voice.

"Of course. I can't believe you doubt me," Reese replied, fingers making a tapping noise as they flew across the keyboard.

Reese had always been technically inclined. He used to build radios from parts, and at eleven, won a science fair when he built his first computer.

Stephan dropped into the chair in front of Ella's sturdy pine desk. The rest of her office incorporated bright pieces from the company's furniture collection.

"What's wrong with your laptop?"

His sister sighed. "I keep getting popups, and the computer constantly freezes. I took it home to get some work done, and I stepped out of my office for two seconds. When I came back, the girls were playing on it."

Reese tapped a button. Finished, he looked up at Ella. "They probably downloaded some malware. Don't worry, this program will clean it up. Next time, keep Hannah and Sophia away from the computer."

"I didn't encourage them to play with it, Reese. When you have kids, you'll understand how difficult it is to watch them twenty-four hours a day. They get into everything within seconds."

"He's not having kids, remember?" Stephan said, spooning yogurt, fruit, and granola into his mouth.

Ella frowned at Stephan. "What are you doing on this floor?"

Stephan set the empty yogurt cup and spoon on the edge of her desk. "I need you to increase the snack budget for the rest of the building. You guys have better snacks up here."

On the executive floor, they had choices like hummus and pita chips and yogurt parfaits. He'd also learned they had a smoothie day, during which an outside company set up in the break room and made smoothies to order.

"I'll keep that in mind. Is that why you came into my office?"

"No, I came to ask you about my work buddy, Roselle."

Two sets of eyes looked at him.

"Stay away from her. Mother likes her," Ella said.

"I like her, too."

His sister arched a brow and Reese shook his head, followed by a little chuckle.

"This isn't a hunting ground. It's a place of business," Ella said.

"Obviously I won't get any help from you."

"She's nice, Stephan."

That much he'd already deduced. He sensed the sassy talk was a front, though he liked the idea of her switching up and not taking crap from anybody, including him. But he needed to go slower with her. Prolonging the wait would only make their coming together sweeter.

"I'm not the boogeyman, Ella. Honestly, when you talk like that, it makes me think you don't love me."

"When you talk like that, it makes me think you don't take this job seriously."

"Why are you such a hard ass?" he asked, annoyed.

"Did you think because you're my brother I'd take it easy on you?"

"You know you're slowly turning into her," Stephan said, referring to their mother.

"Thank you."

"It wasn't a compliment."

"You know what your problem is?"

"I'm sure you'll tell me," he said with a weary sigh.

"You're spoiled," she said.

"No shit, Sherlock."

"Kids, kids, stop fighting," Reese said.

"You be quiet. You're exactly like me, but you're sneaky with your dirt."

"I would very much like to be excluded from this conversation," Reese said.

Stephan rolled his shoulders to release the tension. "Never mind about Roselle. I'll find out about her on my own. Next question. Why did SJ Brands stop expansion into Brazil?"

Ella shrugged. "Mother had someone working on that market, but Marcus, the VP of business development, fired him because he was doing a terrible job. It was right before I left to become a stay-at-home mom. He was never replaced, that I know of. Why?"

"It's a huge market. The largest single market in South America, but our penetration is shallow. We should have a greater presence there, like we do in Argentina, for example."

"Do you have a plan?"

"I have some ideas."

"Stephan, I know you just started, but you have to do better than ideas. You need to do research and come up with a plan and show how it can be implemented before we spend money trying to penetrate that market. You should make that your project. Think of how proud Mother would be, and then you'd be back in her good graces." She flashed a grin.

"I like the way you think."

"You're welcome."

"Now, I need to talk to someone who's aware of trends and can help me with market research. Who has that kind of knowledge?" He tapped his chin. "I know! I'll reach out to Roselle, one of the fashion directors." He smirked and stood.

"Behave, Stephan," Ella warned.

Backing out of her office, he chuckled. "When have I ever?"

WALKING through the reception area on the side of the floor where the creatives worked, Stephan ignored the way the admins looked at him. He was used to women ogling him and talking about his good looks. He used to like it and certainly took advantage. But the compliments got old, and he began to realize that's all they saw —his looks. To them, he was a blank slate. A man without substance.

Maybe they were right. What had he actually done in his life? Even working here was a joke. Although Stephan had an idea for the Brazil market, as his sister so bluntly pointed out, he needed more than an idea. He didn't know how far he wanted to go with this, but he'd look into it. That's where Roselle came in.

A smile spread across his lips as he approached her door. She was knowledgeable and could point him in the right direction for this project. And maybe, just maybe, he'd get back on his mother's good side and leave this position sooner rather than later.

He knocked on Roselle's door.

"Come in," she called.

From out in the hallway, her voice gave him chills. He almost forgot the reason he'd come by. If he didn't have her soon, he might lose his mind.

He walked in, and when she saw him, she popped up from a crouching position beside her desk, holding a magazine in her hand.

With a quick scan, he assessed the office. Damn, it was crowded in here.

"You have a lot of stuff," he said.

"I know it's messy, but people hardly ever come by to talk, and when I want to conduct meetings, I have them in the conference room or meet with the designers one floor below." With an embarrassed grimace, she cast her gaze around the room.

Personally, he didn't like clutter, but his comment was simply an observation. To put her mind at ease, he said, "The mess doesn't bother me. I bet you know where everything is."

"I do. Most of the time," Roselle replied. She placed the magazine on the desk. "How can I help you?"

Today she wore a simple wine-colored cap-sleeved blouse, and her legs were shown off to advantage by a knee-length, loose-fitting skirt with a ruffled hemline. His gaze lingered on her bare legs. How was it possible to have sexy ankles?

He bit his bottom lip and let his gaze travel slowly up her slender body. He could get up under that skirt with ease. One of the best parts of making love to a woman was exploring her body, and he wanted to explore hers—find every mole and drag his tongue along her feminine curves.

With difficulty, Stephan refocused and told her why he'd stopped by.

"Have you talked to Marcus?" she asked.

"Not yet. I need to do some leg work first," he admitted.

Marcus clearly didn't expect much, didn't offer any encouragement, and barely gave him work to do. It was obvious he considered supervising Stephan as more of a babysitting gig.

"What do you want to know?"

Roselle took a seat, and Stephan did, too. For the next twenty minutes, she answered his questions. She explained how Chinese imports dominated the Brazilian market, though she believed there was a place for SJ Brands there. She recited facts and figures and explained notable trends. When they were finished, he was in awe.

"How do you keep all of that information in your brain?"

"When you love what you do, it's easy. And, of course, having someone like your mother as a mentor makes it easier. She's tough but fair and has a wealth of knowledge in her head. The staff doesn't take advantage of her industry knowledge enough. She has an answer for anything I ask. It's amazing."

What he initially thought might be a performance that first day obviously was not. She really did admire his mother.

"I have to admit, I'm a bit surprised you like her so much. You two are nothing alike. My mother's a shark," he said with amusement.

"More of a tiger, I'd say. No one can mess with her, but it's obvious how much she loves you—loves all her children. The way a mother should. Not all mothers are good. Be grateful for the one you have."

She whispered the last part in an odd-toned voice. As if she'd shared too much, her gaze to the left so that he no longer saw her eyes, but he didn't miss the tension in her neck.

That made him wonder, did she not have that type of care and protection with her own family? Which, now that he thought about it, was something he took for granted. It was comforting and reassuring to know he would be taken care of and protected at all costs by a mother who was, as she pointed out, a tiger.

Roselle cleared her throat and stood. "I have a few books and magazines you might want to check out."

She stepped over the pile of magazines beside her desk and walked by him. Stephan followed to an overstuffed bookcase.

"So, you never mentioned if you have a boyfriend," Stephan said casually. His gaze lowered to the way the loose-fitting skirt draped over her hips and pert little bottom.

Roselle glanced over her shoulder and caught him staring. He didn't care if she saw him checking her out. He wanted her to know.

She quickly turned around and studied the books and periodicals stuffed onto the shelves. "Why is that important?"

He let his voice drop an octave, the way women liked. "Just curious. I don't have a girlfriend."

"Have you ever had a girlfriend?" She removed a book and handed it back to him.

"I have. Been a while, though."

The truth was, monogamy held little appeal when it was so easy to get women. It was actually too easy, and over time, he'd become bored and just plain tired.

But who was he going to tell he was tired of running across the same types willing to do any and everything for a night with him? Who was he going to tell he was tired of getting his dick sucked, just by asking? Hell, practically all he had to do was snap his fingers.

When you got tired, you did dumb shit to add excitement and up the ante. One woman wasn't enough, you needed two. Or maybe he slept with three instead of two. The whole thing became a game. Why not four, while he was at it? And they'd let him.

Add the inhibition-lowering effects of alcohol, and nothing was off limits. Nothing was out of bounds. Because he was bored.

"How about you? How long has it been since you've had a serious boyfriend?" Stephan asked.

"It's been a while for me, too."

"Look at that, it's been a while since we've both been in a relationship, and we're both currently single."

"And we're both friends. Maybe we can set each other up."

She was teasing him, but the suggestion that he set her up aggravated the hell out of him. "I don't know any men who are right for you, and I'm not interested in anyone you'd introduce me to."

"You don't know that." She stretched onto her toes, reaching for another book.

His gaze traveled over her figure. She looked light enough to lift against the wall with ease. "I know because I'm only interested in you," he said.

Enough of going slow. Being close to her made him want her more. The scent of her perfume filled his nostrils. It wasn't flowery or musky—more of a natural fragrance like almonds. And he was already semi-erect thinking about them naked and her legs in the air while he screwed her on top of every book and magazine on her desk.

Roselle slowly turned to face him, holding two thick catalogs against her chest.

"We work together."

"So what?"

"That's an issue."

"Not for me."

"You're the boss's son. Not to mention, you're not my type."

"You sure about that?"

"Yes." She stared defiantly into his eyes.

"Strange, because I see the way you look at me, and I'm pretty sure you want me. I've had years of practice reading the signs from women."

"Give it up, Stephan. I'm not interested." She thrust the catalogs at him, and he took them.

He paused for a minute. "So you say. Thanks for the books, friend."

With a grin, he left her office.

CHAPTER 7

*W*ell after the close of business, Stephan strolled into his mother's office, expecting her to be alone if she was in there. Instead, Roselle sat before her desk, and his mother slammed the desk phone into its cradle.

"Well, that's that," she said in a tight voice.

"What's wrong?" Stephan asked.

Roselle twisted around to look at him.

"Jacob was supposed to go on the Paris trip with Roselle tomorrow but he no longer can. I absolutely want someone from business development to accompany her. Jacob had a death in his family, and I can't reach anyone else on the team. Not even Marcus. Why isn't anyone answering their phone!"

"Marcus can't go, anyway. He's going to that event in Las Vegas."

"Is there anyone left in your department?"

"Last person left about thirty minutes ago." He'd been in his office, pouring over the books Roselle had loaned him last week. He'd come up here to this floor to get a snack, and decided to see if his mother was in and say hi.

"Who else can go on such short notice? Her flight leaves tomorrow." Sylvie sighed and pressed a hand to her temple.

"I can go with her," Stephan said.

Roselle stiffened, and his mother frowned.

"I'm sorry, my darling, but you don't have enough experience."

Stephan braced his hands on the back of the chair next to Roselle. "We're information-gathering, not closing a deal. Besides, Rue de la Mode is trying to impress us, not the other way around, and Roselle will be there. She's sharp and has an incredible memory."

His mother looked between them.

Stephan pressed home his advantage. "I speak French fluently, so you won't need a translator. It's one day of meetings and checking out the stores. That's it. Roselle and I can bring back the information to you and the rest of the team. Or do you prefer to wait and see who's available, when none of them might be? Meanwhile, I'm available right now. We can finalize the flight details tonight, so Roselle and I are ready to go tomorrow."

Sylvie sighed again. "You're right. We're information-gathering at this point. Roselle, Stephan is your new partner. This might work out better. As he mentioned, he speaks French fluently, and he knows his way around Paris. You'll be in good hands."

"Great. I guess we're all set," Roselle said evenly.

"Make sure the travel department knows about the change —*tonight*. I don't want any hiccups tomorrow."

"I will." Roselle stood.

"Well, now that I've saved the day, I'll head over to the break room and see what snacks you all have for me to indulge in," Stephan said.

He turned to follow Roselle out, but his mother's voice stopped him.

"Stephan, wait a minute. I'd like to talk to you privately."

Uh-oh. He turned slowly back around but couldn't read her expression.

"Roselle, close the door on your way out, please." Sylvie leaned back in her chair and watched Stephan.

43

Roselle did as she was asked, and Stephan came to stand before his mother like a man before a tribunal.

"I was told that you and Roselle have been eating lunch together every day. Is that correct?"

"Not every day. We've only eaten together twice," Stephan said defensively. *Who was talking to his mother about him?*

"Only lunch?" She arched a groomed brow.

"Of course, Mother. We only have an hour." He flashed a grin.

"A lot can happen in an hour."

His grin disappeared. He didn't want to think about what she meant. Despite his mother having four children, he preferred to think neither of his parents knew anything about sex, especially with each other. "True, but we only have lunch."

Sylvie stood and came around the desk to stand before him. "I like the idea of you traveling to France to work with Roselle. It will be a good experience for you, and you can make sure she has a good time—sees the sights and all that, as much as one can see in such a short period of time. I like her and want to make sure she takes time to enjoy herself. I don't get the impression that she does that very often."

Interesting how both women admired each other.

"Please be on your best behavior."

"Aren't I always?"

"No, you're not. Don't make me regret sending you on this trip."

"I'm shocked you'd say that."

She arched her brow again, making it very clear that she did not fall for his phony act of being offended. "I love you, Stephan, flaws and all, but make no mistake, I do know what your flaws are. I should have told you this before, but keep away from the models."

"You make it sound as if I can't control myself. And by the way, I haven't seen any models since I've been here." Sadly.

"Tell me you will not sleep with the models."

"You will not sleep with the models." Sylvie's lips tightened.

"Oh, you mean me. I will not sleep with any of the models," he amended.

"I will not sleep with any employee of SJ Brands or SJ Media."

His smile wavered, and his mind immediately went to Roselle. He had plans for her. "Not any? That's a lot of people." At her stern expression, he reluctantly recited, "I will not sleep with any employee of SJ Brands or SJ Media."

"Good. And to make sure that you don't do any of the above, I'll add a condition to our agreement. If you break your pledge to me, I will change the date on the disbursement of the money in your trust fund." She walked around her desk.

"What! That's my money. January first, after I turn thirty, I get my money."

In addition to being a savvy businesswoman, Sylvie was a calculating investor, hiring only the best minds to manage her assets. She had set up trust funds for each of her children, which ensured that on January first after they turned thirty, they each received over a billion dollars in cash, real estate, stocks, and other assets. He'd been counting on that money to make him independent of her purse strings.

She crossed her legs and tapped her fingers on the arm of the chair. "It's not your money until it's disbursed to you. One call to my attorney and I can have the date changed."

"But you won't do that," Stephan stated, though it was really a question.

"When have you ever known me to make idle threats?"

Never. His stomach heaved in panic mode.

"Behave yourself, and you won't have anything to worry about it. I especially want you to stay away from Roselle, is that clear? She's a nice young woman, and I like having her around."

"I heard you, Mother," he grumbled.

"Excellent. All you have to do is exercise self-control, Stephan. If you have no control over your impulses, how can I trust that you're mature enough to handle that amount of wealth? You may squander it. Prove to me that you've changed, and you'll get the proceeds from the trust on January first, as planned."

She was serious. He saw it in her eyes. *Goddammit.*

"I can do that," he said evenly, smiling through gritted teeth.

"I know you can. Now, you should get home and prepare. Maybe take the day off tomorrow. You're leaving for Paris tomorrow in the evening."

"Good night."

"Good night, my darling," she said cheerily.

Stephan stalked out of her office, muttering a stream of curse words under his breath.

As much as he wanted Roselle, no way was he missing out on a partial disbursement of his inheritance. His sisters had already collected theirs, and he was damn sure going to collect his, too.

* * *

"Hɪ, ᴀᴜɴᴛɪᴇ," Roselle said to her great-aunt, Betty Parker.

"Hey, baby," her great-aunt said.

Her clothes were much looser on her now, and her eyes weren't as bright, but that smile could light up the darkest night. People said Roselle had inherited her great-aunt's smile, which was a huge compliment if that were true.

She bent down and hugged the older woman's frail body in the wheelchair. Betty sat by herself on the back porch of the nursing home where she been living for the past four years. Roselle knew it frustrated her that she was no longer able to take care of herself, but the facility became a necessity after she fell at home and was unable to call for help. Roselle found her over twenty-four hours later, dehydrated and stinking of urine.

Thanks to a good salary and strict budgeting, she was able to place her great-aunt in Covent Gardens and no longer had to worry about her when they were apart. She usually came to visit on the weekend but made a special trip today because she was leaving the country tomorrow.

Her relationship with Betty was more that of mother and daughter. Betty had taken care of Roselle since she was sixteen years old when her mother sent her away after the sexual assault that rocked their community. Betty had held her while she cried and wiped her tears. If it weren't for her Aunt Betty, she'd have no one in the world, so she treasured their relationship, holding onto it tight.

She'd only seen her mother a few times since she left, and not at all in the past five years. Their relationship was irretrievably broken, and her heart grieved that it would never be repaired.

"What you got there?" Betty asked, pointing her finger at the box in Roselle's hand.

Roselle sat down and crossed her legs. "A little something for you." She lifted off the cover and pulled out a colorful silk scarf. Her aunt loved scarves.

Betty's eyes widened in excitement. "Is that a Sylvie design?"

Roselle nodded. "This one I designed myself, and it's only in the most exclusive boutiques around the country."

"Oh, my, my, my. Ethel is going to be so jealous."

Roselle laughed.

Until Betty came along, Ethel won bragging rights at the nursing home in the grandchildren department because her granddaughter was one of the youngest Superior Court judges in the country. However, there wasn't much to show off except the occasional times her granddaughter's name appeared in the newspaper.

On the other hand, Betty continuously bragged that her grandniece was first a fashion designer and now a fashion director at one of the top brands in the world, and occasionally she gifted Betty with items from the various lines. Roselle had to admit that she thought their rivalry was hilarious and enjoyed fueling it by bringing in clothing and accessories her aunt could show off to her friends.

"Don't rub it in her face too much." Roselle looped the scarf around her aunt's neck.

Betty lifted her shoulders into the delicate cloth. "It's so soft."

"It's pure silk."

Betty took one end and rubbed her cheek. "This is so nice. Thank you, baby." Her thin fingers reached over and patted Roselle's hand.

"Glad you like it."

It gave her so much pleasure to do something so small for her aunt, particularly after everything she had done for her. Thanks to Betty, she earned a degree in fashion design. Thanks to Betty, she didn't wilt away into depression.

Her stint at SJ Brands started only five years ago as an in-house designer. She'd been nervous and unsure of herself, but a couple of years in, Sylvie had shown particular interest in her and changed her whole life. Now she oversaw two of the fashion lines, *and* she was on her way to Paris to work on a deal Sylvie had handpicked her for.

Aside from visiting her aunt, her job was her life, and she flourished in a career that she loved. But there were times she yearned for more, yet didn't dare reach for what she wanted.

"You ready for Paris?" Betty asked.

"I've been ready. I asked Miss Sylvie if I could stay an extra day, and she said that I should definitely do that and do some sightseeing."

"That's so exciting! I can't wait to see your pictures. So it sounds like you're ready to go."

"Yes. I have my passport, and I'm staying in the company apartment." Roselle pulled up the photo gallery on her phone. "This is the apartment I'll be staying in."

"That's so beautiful." Betty squeezed Roselle's hand. "I'm so proud of you and everything you've accomplished. I know there is much more for you to do."

"Miss Sylvie's son, Stephan, will be coming with me."

"I thought his name was Reese?"

"Reese works in IT. Stephan is her older son. He's new to the company and started in business development."

"Well, that's nice. What's he like?"

Roselle shrugged nonchalantly though her pulse rate had picked up. "We get along fine. We've had lunch together a couple of times. I won't need a translator with him there, and he's been to Paris before, so I'll practically have my own tour guide."

"Sounds like everything is working out perfectly. You're going to have a wonderful time!"

Roselle laughed, the thought of Paris invoking excitement and a sense of adventure. "I know I will. It's Paris!"

CHAPTER 8

*S*tephan tucked Roselle's carry-on bag into the overhead storage compartment. He wore dark denim pants and a fitted gray T-shirt that stretched across his chest and cupped the biceps in his arms. Roselle struggled not to stare. He looked good in anything.

He stepped aside so she could sit down next to the window, and she settled into the spacious first-class seat. She was on her way to Paris! The City of Light, the City of Love. Excitement thrummed through her veins as she looked out at the tarmac where airport employees hustled around, directing air traffic or loading luggage onto the planes.

Beside her, Stephan grumbled something. "What did you say?" she asked.

He leaned away from the aisle as other passengers came aboard and walked past.

"This is ridiculous," he muttered.

"What's ridiculous?"

He stretched his legs and moaned. "Having to fly commercial."

She gave him her full attention. "How do you normally fly?"

"One of the family's planes or I charter a flight."

"Why didn't you charter a flight this time?" Roselle asked.

Stephan gave her a sidelong glance. "Honestly, because I can't afford to throw around money like that anymore. I'm on a budget." There was quite a bit of bitterness in his voice.

"I guess this isn't a self-imposed budget?"

"Smart and funny. You're quite the catch."

Roselle rolled her eyes. "You're always joking. Are you ever serious?"

"Who says I'm joking? You are smart, and you are funny. You don't think so?"

Was he making fun of her? "I'm not funny."

His eyebrows raised. "Oh, so you think you're smart?"

"I—"

"I'm kidding. I'm picking on you." His face grew serious. "In case you didn't know, you're smart, funny, pretty, and sexy, and I'm dead serious about that."

His voice had dropped so low, she felt the vibrations deep between her thighs as if he'd rested his mouth there while he spoke.

Roselle swallowed. "Nice line," she said quietly.

He trapped her with his gaze, and her heart raced as she waited for his reply. His response shouldn't matter so much, but it did.

"I say a lot of things, sometimes true, sometimes not true. I'm not perfect, I've done a lot of crap I'm not proud of. But I've been honest about my interest in you from the beginning. And you've made it plain that you're not interested. I have to admit, it bruised my ego because I'm not used to being turned down."

"So have you finally given up?"

He rested the back of his head against the seat and closed his eyes. His jaw grew tight. "Yeah. It's in my best interest to stay away from you."

Roselle blinked. She hadn't expected that answer. Flooded by unexpected disappointment, she returned her attention to the activity outside. Airport employees continued milling about, and a plane came cruising in and landed on the runway.

She had wanted him to give up, but now that he had, she didn't feel as relieved as she should.

"Got any big plans for tomorrow?" Stephan asked.

Roselle shrugged. "Nothing much. My birthday is the day after tomorrow, and staying an extra day in Paris is my gift to myself."

"Your birthday is the day after tomorrow?" Stephan stared at her in disbelief.

"Yes."

"How old will you be?'

"Thirty."

He gaped at her. "That's a milestone birthday. Why didn't you say something before?"

She shrugged. "I don't make a big deal about my birthday."

"What does that even mean? No party? No cake?"

"I don't need any of that."

"Come on. We could have made plans."

"These are my plans. I'm going to spend the day in Paris."

His eyebrows elevated. "My birthdays are a week-long celebration."

"That's not too bad. I know people who celebrate all month long."

"So do I, but that's too much celebrating, even for me." He frowned. "But you have to do something for your big day. I know, why don't you come out to the club with me tonight? I'm meeting a friend at a popular nightclub. Great place, lively music, fine crowd. You'd like it."

She wasn't much for going to clubs and partying. "I'll think about it."

"Come on, you can't stay in the apartment all night."

"I don't plan to, but I want to at least take a picture in front of the Eiffel Tower."

"Of course. You can't go to Paris without seeing it up close, but our apartment is in the seventh arrondissement, in the heart of the Left Bank. From any of the windows, you'll be able to see La Tour

Eiffel. Come with me to the club, and I'll make sure you see La Tour Eiffel up close tomorrow."

La Tour Eiffel. That was the first time Roselle had heard him speak French, and with a perfect accent. It was so darn sexy.

"I'll think about it," she said again.

"I'm not giving up until you say yes."

He angled his head toward her a little bit, and a mischievous smile crossed his face, and of course, she blushed. He unnerved her and made her feel out of sorts, as always, without trying.

"I'll think about it," she repeated.

Stephan sighed. "All right. Make sure you get some sleep on this flight. The time change will mess you up. When we arrive in France, it'll be six in the morning, and our first meeting is at nine."

"I can't sleep. I'm too excited."

"Trust me, even a short nap will help." He rested his head against the seat back again and closed his eyes.

Roselle studied his profile. She didn't think she'd be able to sleep on the trans-Atlantic flight. Not when she was so eager to see Paris, and certainly not with the man beside her taking up so much of her thoughts.

* * *

ROSELLE DID sleep on the plane and snapped photos from the airport to their final destination.

"We are here," their driver Sébastien said. He was a tall, swarthy-skinned man with prominent muscles under his black uniform, who looked like he doubled as a bodyguard and probably did.

They rolled to a stop in front of the building. Sébastien exited the vehicle and opened the door on Roselle's side, giving her a helping hand as she descended from the car. As Stephan also climbed out, the driver retrieved their bags and escorted them to the front door where he punched in a code.

Inside, he left them after a thin man about Roselle's height immediately approached. He wore a black vest, black slacks, and a white short-sleeved shirt. From the briefing she'd received, she knew he was their butler.

"Monsieur Brooks, Mademoiselle Parker, welcome." He clasped Stephan's hand and then hers.

"Giles, you haven't changed a bit," Stephan said.

The other man laughed. "You are kind. I have a few more gray hairs since the last time I saw you, and I've had too much bread and pastries." He patted his flat stomach.

If that's what bread and pastries did to one's body, she should incorporate them more into her diet.

Giles lifted their bags.

"Never too much of that," Stephan said, following behind Giles.

The three of them squeezed into a small elevator, and Roselle stood in front of Stephan. She was acutely aware of him—his presence, his height. When they exited, they walked down the hall, and Giles let them into the apartment. When Roselle walked in, her mouth fell open. The apartment had apparently gone through a renovation.

The decor was classic French, light and bright with white or cream-colored chairs and sofas, gold drapes at the windows, and gold-framed mirrors on the walls.

"It's two floors?" she said, turning to look at Stephan.

He nodded. "One bedroom upstairs and one downstairs. Which do you want?"

"I'll take the one upstairs," she replied.

"We give the lady whatever she wishes," Giles said.

"Always," Stephan agreed.

Giles took her carry-on up the stairs, and Stephan took his through a door behind the stairs. Roselle took her time alone to get acquainted with the apartment.

She walked through the sitting room to the dining area where there was a plate of colorful macaroons waiting under a clear glass cover, and a vase of fresh flowers probably purchased from the neighborhood flower shop they'd passed on the way in.

There were two large windows—one in the sitting area and the other in the dining area. She stepped over to the one near the table and looked down onto the street. Because of the early hour, most of the shops were still closed, and only a few people traveled around on foot. In the distance, the grandeur of the wrought-iron Eiffel Tower loomed so close she almost believed if she stretched out her hand she'd touch it. Her face broke into a wide grin.

"Is there anything I can get for you, mademoiselle?" Giles asked.

Roselle turned around at the sound of his voice. "No, I'm fine."

"If you need anything, please do not hesitate to call me. Pick up the phone there and dial." He gave her the number. "Day or night."

"Day or night?" Roselle repeated.

"Yes, that's correct. I am here to make your stay as comfortable as possible." He smiled at her.

"Thanks, Giles," Stephan said, standing near the door.

Giles walked back over to him, and both men spoke French for several minutes. Then Stephan handed him a few euros, and Giles left them alone.

The finality of the door closing behind him made her think about how she'd be in this house, alone, with Stephan, for the next two nights.

* * *

THE TWO MORNING meetings went well. Then they visited a couple of Rue de la Mode stores, ending with the flagship store, where the reps planned to launch the Sylvie brand products. The last visit took approximately one hour, during which they talked to employees and checked out the front and back of the store. Roselle discussed how SJ Brands would fit in with the rest of the brands they carried. By the end of the meeting when they broke for lunch,

Roselle felt confident that Sylvie would be pleased with the location. They shook hands with their hosts and then left.

Sébastien picked them up outside and took them a couple of miles away to a restaurant where Parisians leisurely dined on salads and baguette sandwiches and sipped wine. Roselle let Stephan order for her, and he chose a meal that consisted of a side salad and something called a *croque monsieur*, which was a leveled-up version of a ham sandwich made with Gruyère cheese and covered in a creamy béchamel before toasting under the broiler or cooking on a griddle.

"Well, what do you think?" Stephan asked, inclining his head toward her plate.

"Delicious." She crossed her eyes and he chuckled, leaning back in his chair.

"That good, huh?"

"I can't go back to a regular ham sandwich."

"Wait till you have a Nutella crepe."

"That sounds good, but I don't want to be greedy," she said, though the idea was tempting.

"You're in Paris, you have to have the full experience. Crepes are part of the Paris experience."

"And bakeries, apparently. They're everywhere."

"The whole city should be obese, but they're not."

She nodded. "Yeah, and the portions are smaller here."

Stephan folded his arms and studied her from across the table, his eyes lit up in amusement.

"Why are you looking at me like that?" she asked, suddenly self-conscious.

"You're noticing things that I take for granted. I've been here so many times I don't pay attention to the differences as much."

She leaned across the table and whispered, "And I can't believe people actually do walk around with baguettes in their hand. I took a picture to show my aunt when I get back."

Stephan did a full-on laugh this time. A man's laugh. Throaty and masculine, it made her fingers and toes tingle.

"She's going to live vicariously through you, I guess?" he asked.

"Yes. Definitely."

Stephan's phone rang, and when he answered, he started speaking in fluent French. Listening to him, she wished she understood what he was saying. He was definitely animated and very sexy. The accent and his intonation completely changed. Sleeping with the boss's son was probably high on the list of things one should never do, yet hearing him talk in another language and hearing his easy laughter tempted her resolve.

Stephan hung up the phone. "That was my buddy Franck. He wanted to confirm that I'm going to the club tonight. You have to come. It'll be a great way to let loose, and you said you wanted to see the Champs-Élysées, right?"

"I do."

"The club is on a side street off the Champs-Élysées. They play all kinds of music—hip-hop, rock, funk, Afrobeats. A lot of indie artists but also well-known artists from here and the States. To be honest, it's basically a tourist trap with a high cover charge and overpriced drinks, but a good number of French-speaking people go there, too. Franck's uncle is the manager. You game?"

She hadn't been to a club in years and wasn't entirely sure she wanted to go now, but Stephan's roguish grin enticed her.

"I'm game," she said.

CHAPTER 9

*A*fter their afternoon meetings, Roselle told Stephan she'd explore the neighborhood on her own. He'd been hesitant to leave her at first, but she insisted that she'd be fine for a while until they met up again to go to the club. He had friends he should be spending time with instead of babysitting her.

It was clear he felt some responsibility for her, and since she didn't speak the language, it was nice having him around, but she wanted time to herself—away from him. While he was still friendly, his behavior toward her had changed, and she didn't know how to process that. He'd obviously lost interest.

The same could not be said for her. Spending the entire day with Stephan had been a harrowing experience because of her intense attraction to him. He had a certain pull, and she couldn't deny wanting to stay in his orbit. So getting a break where he went off by himself and she went off by herself, was a welcome relief and a chance to clear her head.

She took her time exploring the neighborhood, walking along the cobblestoned streets and snapping photos of the buildings. Along the way, she browsed the specialty shops, careful to say *"Bonjour"* upon entering each one, as recommended in her reading material.

She spent only a few minutes at the *boucherie*, butcher shop, and didn't buy anything. At the *boulangerie*, bakery, she purchased a delicious little strawberry tart and tucked it in her purse to snack on later. At the *fromagerie*, cheese shop, the owner talked animatedly about his seasonal bests in halting English. She left with a small selection that included sharp gorgonzola, creamy sheep's cheese from the French Basque country, and a jar of strawberry lavender jam as an accompaniment.

One of her last stops was a boutique where she purchased an outfit for later. Stephan had warned her that getting into a popular club meant dressing well, and that did not necessarily mean wearing tight or short clothing. The dress she chose was a splurge but one she didn't regret.

That night in her room, she squirted perfume on her neck and wrists and pinned her hair at her nape, showing off the gold earrings she brought on the trip. They went perfectly with the metallic gold of the shift dress, which featured a matching band that tied around her waist. The long, sheer sleeves cinched around her wrists with a balloon effect, and the hemline fell to her knees. She paired the outfit with strappy sandals with thick heels that were comfortable for walking. If Stephan's intense stare was anything to go by when she walked down the stairs, she'd done well.

"You look great," he said when she stopped in front of him.

"So do you."

His outfit consisted of dark gray chinos, a navy-blue blazer, and a white collarless shirt under it. His only accessory was a Vacheron Constantin brand watch with a brown leather band, which easily cost as much as her annual salary.

"Let's go," he said, and let her walk ahead of him.

Sébastien dropped them off in the middle of the Champs-Élysées. The busy avenue was over a mile long and filled with tourists and residents strolling the sidewalks on both sides and checking out the souvenir shops, car showrooms, restaurants, and high-end clothing stores like Sylvie and Louis Vuitton.

They stopped at the Sylvie store and introduced themselves to the workers, letting them know they were from the US head office. When the staff learned Stephan was Sylvie Johnson's son, they became excited, and she and Stephan had to practically tear themselves away, or they might not have been able to leave.

Roselle asked Stephan to take a photo of her with the backdrop of the Arc de Triomphe, a massive monument on the western end of the avenue which had been commissioned by Napoleon. Then they took a side street and approached Le Rêve nightclub on foot, and Roselle was doubly glad she'd bought a new outfit.

Women of all races were lined up outside wearing stylish, figure-hugging outfits that flattered their bodies while showing off their fashion sense.

Stephan took her hand in his and led the way past the line to the front door.

His warm clasp made her belly tighten. A quick glance at his profile suggested he hadn't experienced a charge the way she did, and once again, she was disappointed in his lack of interest.

The men and women waiting outside were a mix of college-age and young professionals who stared at them as they walked past. At the front door, the bouncer's face spread into a wide smile when he saw Stephan. They spoke for a few minutes in French before the guy took a quick look at Roselle and let them past.

They entered the crowded club, whose tall ceiling consisted of red and white lights that hung from wrought iron in a crisscrossed design. On the opposite side of the building, a deejay wearing headphones over a backward-turned cap stood on stage hunched over turntables and surrounded by an entourage of men and women. Gyrating bodies crowded the area around the stage, dancing to an unfamiliar hip-hop song as the artist rapped in French.

Out of nowhere, a tall, elegant woman with a familiar face approached and stood directly in their path.

"*Bonsoir*, Stephan. How long are you in Paris?" she asked in a

British accent, speaking loud enough to be heard above the thumping music. She placed a hand on his crotch and squeezed.

Stephan grunted as if in pain. "Not long." He carefully removed the woman's hand from between his legs.

"Too bad," she said with a pretty pout.

That's when Roselle remembered she was a top British model known only by her first name, Namia. In high heels, she was as tall as Stephan with thick lips set between high cheekbones and skin as smooth and dark as garnet stone. Coupled with the vibrant blue wig she wore, she was head-turning with her graceful movements. Absolutely stunning, but downright rude.

"Excuse me," Roselle said, stepping closer to Stephan. What was she, invisible? "We're here together."

Namia flicked her gaze up and down Roselle's smaller form. "Oh, really?" Her gaze met Stephan's again, seeking confirmation.

He flung an arm around Roselle's neck and squeezed her closer to his hard body. Her breasts tightened at the contact.

"I'm taken," Stephan said.

The model studied him for a moment and then arched one eyebrow. "How long are you and your friend here?"

"We leave the day after tomorrow."

"I see. Well..." She grasped the front of Stephan's shirt and yanked him closer, forcing Roselle to stumble forward, too, because his arm remained around her neck. "In case you've forgotten what I'm capable of..."

She leaned in and whispered in Stephan's ear. Roselle didn't hear what she said, but the reminder made him gulp.

Namia stood back and dragged her palm slowly down his chest to smooth out the wrinkles she created. She tossed a hungry look at Roselle that made her press closer into Stephan's side.

"Call me. I only need an hour. And your friend can come, too."

With that, Namia turned on her high heels and two burly men that Roselle hadn't noticed before—probably bodyguards—followed in her wake

"What the hell? Holy crap, she's aggressive!" Roselle said.

"You have no idea. That was her holding back because we're in public. Thanks for being a buffer." He kept his arm around her shoulders, looking down at her as if…as if she belonged there, tucked into his side.

She'd responded with such fervor because seeing another woman grab his privates as if they belonged to her made her enraged and she had to speak up. "Does she always do that, just… grab you like that?"

He shrugged. "Not always."

"You shouldn't allow it. She has no right to do that."

"It's not a big—"

"It *is* a big deal. You're a person, not a piece of meat," Roselle said firmly.

He arched a brow. "I guess you're right," he said slowly, studying her for a moment.

"Your boundaries need to be respected just as much as anybody else's."

One corner of his mouth twisted upward into a sexy smile. He bent his head to her ear. "Thanks for looking out for me."

"You're welcome." Roselle edged away from him. She'd become too comfortable hugged up against him. "By the way, what did she mean by saying that I can join you? She doesn't know me."

"She doesn't have to know you. She liked what she saw."

Her eyes widened, and he laughed.

"What kind of people do you know? Is your other friend like that?"

"Franck is nothing like that. He's cool people. And there he is."

A man about their age with swarthy skin and a mop of curly dark hair approached. He and Stephan slapped hands. "Have you been here long?" he asked in accented English.

"Just got here. This is Roselle."

"You did not tell me she was so beautiful. Hello, Roselle. I am Franck Bongo, French by way of Gabon. *Enchanté*." He lifted her hand and kissed the back of it.

"Don't start that French lover shit," Stephan said, shooting his friend a dark look.

"I want her to have the full French experience," Franck said.

"Then greet her properly."

"He is jealous, this one." Franck jabbed a finger in Stephan's direction.

Roselle giggled. She liked him already.

Franck leaned in and gave her the customary double kiss, one on each cheek. "With a name like Roselle, you speak French, *oui?*" he asked.

"Does *bonjour* and *au revoir* count?"

He gave a hearty laugh. "So you're not like our friend here, who speaks many languages?"

"Many languages? Come on, now," Stephan said.

"Why be modest? You speak six languages."

"Three. The rest…let's say I can get by."

"Pfft! No, it is not true. He speaks French, English, Portuguese, Spanish, German, and a little Dutch."

Roselle looked at Stephan. She had no idea.

"My German sucks. I need to get better." Stephan shrugged.

"He is too modest. But anyway, you do not need to speak French because I speak English. We have fun tonight, okay?" Franck said.

"Okay," Roselle said. She appreciated his friendliness.

"*Allons-y, mes amis.*"

They followed him, skirting the dance floor before climbing three steps to an elevated area that was roped off. A man standing guard in a black suit lifted the rope and Franck went to sit on a chair while Roselle and Stephan sat on a red velvet couch. A wrought iron railing further separated them from the crowd they looked at below.

Soon, drinks and food were ordered, and Roselle relaxed into the evening, ready for a more casual experience during her trip. She would never have done this on her own. While she was sorry Jacob had to cancel for such grave reasons, she was happy that she had the opportunity to see another side of the city, courtesy of Stephan.

CHAPTER 10

$\mathcal{T}$he deejay lowered the music and spoke French into the mic. Since they'd been there, he'd alternated between French and English to the international crowd. Now her ears picked up Stephan's name in his thick accent.

"...Stephan Brooks here tonight. Where are you, brother?"

A white spotlight flashed over the crowd.

"Oh no," Stephan muttered.

"What's wrong?" Roselle asked.

The light settled on them—specifically, on Stephan. Confused, Roselle stepped back. The deejay continued talking and pointed at Stephan, and cheers of encouragement erupted from the crowd. Because he spoke in French, Roselle had no idea what was being said.

"*Venez!* Come on up!" the deejay said into the microphone.

"Go! *Allez!*" Franck said with a huge grin.

The crowd continued hollering and cheering. What was going on?

"He wants me to come up there and deejay," Stephan said, speaking loud enough to be heard over the chanting crowd.

Stephan lifted a hand to indicate he'd come up and the crowd roared again. Then the spotlight disappeared, and the music volume increased.

"You deejay?" Roselle asked in shock. He was a man of many talents.

Stephan shrugged nonchalantly. "I haven't been on the decks in over a year, but I have turntables and other equipment at home that I still play around with. It's just a hobby."

"He's good. He's done some very important parties, and they pay a lot to have him guest deejay," Franck explained.

"How much is a lot?" Roselle asked.

"Fifty," Stephan replied.

"Dollars?" Roselle asked, frowning.

"Fifty thousand dollars," Franck corrected.

"*A night*? Fifty—are you kidding me?"

Stephan chuckled and shrugged again. "Top deejays make five and ten times that amount."

"I'm in the wrong business," Roselle muttered.

Stephan pointed at Franck. "I know you did this, and I'm gonna get you for putting me on the spot. I should send your uncle an invoice."

Franck didn't lose his wide grin.

"I'll be back. Wish me luck," Stephan said to Roselle. He tossed his blazer on the sofa, revealing the white shirt that showed off his lean torso and broad chest, and walked away. He took his time going up on stage, moving with lazy elegance like he had all the time in the world.

She watched as he chatted with the house deejay and studied the equipment. A few minutes later, he stood behind the turntables, and the other guy went offstage. Holding the headphones to one ear, an adorable frown of concentration creased his brow as he hunched over the equipment.

As the other song wound down, Stephan spoke French into the mic, and the crowd cheered. Then he spoke in English. "Thirty minutes of hip-hop. Are you ready, Le Rêve!"

The audience screamed.

Roselle didn't recognize the next song, but the beat had her tapping her feet. If Stephan was at all nervous, he didn't show it. For the next thirty minutes, he played a mashup of American and French hip-hop artists, moving seamlessly between songs. He was so smooth, his head and shoulders bouncing in time to the beat.

Next to her at the railing, Franck alternated between sipping his drink and yelling out the lyrics to the songs. The partygoers were enjoying themselves, hands in the air, their bodies meshed close together as they moved to the beat and also recited the words to the current song.

At one point, Stephan's gaze met hers, and he winked at her. It was his way of acknowledging her in the midst of all the partying and the women on stage, several of whom eyed him in a way that suggested they'd willingly sneak back-stage if he asked.

Roselle smiled at him, and then something happened that she didn't expect. Stephan lowered the volume on the music and spoke to everyone in French, then translated in English. "It's well after midnight, and there's one thing I have to do before I leave the stage. I have a friend here with me tonight, and it's her birthday."

No, no. What was he doing?

"She doesn't like attention, so I'm not going to put her on the spot. But if you don't mind, can I get everyone in here to sing 'Happy Birthday' to her?"

Everyone in the place screamed out their agreement to participate.

"We're in France, so let's do it in French. *Joyeux anniversaire*, on the count of three. *Un, deux, trois... Joyeux anniversaire...*"

Stephan completely stopped the music, and led the entire club in an *a cappella* version of "Happy Birthday" in French. Roselle stood at the railing blinking back tears while over a thousand people sang to her. Their voices raised up to the ceiling and filled every corner of the club, in a beautiful serenade she'd never forget.

When they were finished, Franck placed an arm around her and gave her a quick squeeze. Choked up, Roselle couldn't respond. Stephan was no longer looking at her. He'd put on another song and was in a conversation with the original deejay, who'd returned to the stage.

He had no idea what he'd done tonight. He'd given her one of the best birthday gifts ever.

* * *

CARRYING two shot glasses of liquor, Stephan returned to the VIP section. Roselle was the only one there.

The set had run longer than thirty minutes because once he loosened up, he didn't want to leave the stage. Getting back on the controller and mixing songs in front of a crowd had given him such a rush, he might start doing a few shows a year, just for the hell of it.

"Where's Franck?" He handed Roselle a shot glass.

"He saw someone he needed to catch up with."

"Female?"

"Yes." She looked up at him through her lashes. "You didn't have to have everyone sing happy birthday to me."

"You want me to have them take it back?" he asked.

She laughed. "No. It was really nice. Thank you."

The idea came to him out of the blue. Knowing that she didn't make a big deal about her birthday bothered him, and for a second, he worried he'd overstepped, but seeing her face now, he knew he'd done the right thing. She was glowing, and he felt pretty damn good that he was the reason for that glow.

"What is this?" she asked, holding up the glass.

"Kamikaze—vodka, triple sec, and lime juice. Bottoms up, birthday girl."

He clinked his glass against hers, and they both tossed back the drinks. Roselle grimaced, but he savored the taste as it went down smooth.

"You're not used to drinking, I take it?"

Roselle did a little shiver. "Wine, mostly. That was strong."

"But you liked it."

She bit the corner of her lip. "I did," she admitted, almost shyly.

He'd help her loosen up before the night was over.

Stephen rested his forearms on the metal railing and looked down at the dancing crowd. The energy in the club was contagious, with lights flashing over bodies jostling in time to the music.

Roselle leaned her hip against the railing and faced him. "By the way, you did good up there. How was it after a year-long absence?"

"Like riding a bike. I forgot how much fun deejaying was."

"You plan to get back into it?"

"Nah. It was fun, but I don't need to do it all the time. Maybe every now and again. It was nice for a change of pace. So, I haven't seen you dance all night. What's up with that?" He wanted to see her moves in that little gold dress she wore.

She shrugged.

"Are you going to dance?"

"I'm not." She ran a finger back and forth along the black metal.

Stephan straightened. "Why, you tired?"

"Surprisingly, I'm wide awake."

"In that case, dance with me."

She seemed to shrink right before his eyes. "No way."

"Why not?"

"I don't really dance."

"You will tonight. Let loose and enjoy yourself. You're in Paris, baby. It's okay to have a little fun."

She gnawed the side of her mouth and looked out at the crowd. "I don't want everyone looking at me up here."

"Then let's go down there."

Stephan didn't give Roselle a chance to decline. He took her hand and led the way down the steps.

The deejay had transitioned to a banging Afrobeats mix. Dancing backward, Stephan gently drew her into the middle of the dancers. Stiff and barely moving, she glanced around nervously at the nearby clubbers enjoying themselves. Men and women dropped low or gyrated their hips to the music, grinding on each other as they simulated sex acts with their clothes on.

Meanwhile, Stephan and Roselle barely moved, their steps awkward and not in sync. He stepped closer and held both of her hands. With coaxing movements, he directed her attention to him and guided her in time to the beat.

"Relax. No one's looking at you," he whispered in her ear. He placed both hands on her hips.

Her fingers curled into the front of his shirt. "You sure?" she asked.

Standing so close, he was playing with fire. Every breath he took was filled with the scent of her skin, her perfume. He'd had a hard time being good all day, watching her enjoy herself. Wondering what her lips tasted like as she licked Nutella from the corner of her mouth. It wasn't only her physical attributes that attracted him. Her mind was sexy as hell, too. Observing her talking with the reps had been an unexpected turn-on, her intellect on display as she recited numbers and listed the expectations of SJ Brands.

"Positive. I'm the only one looking at you."

Her expressive brown eyes darkened, and his stomach knotted. Yeah, he was definitely playing with fire.

Stephan directed her steps, and as she relaxed, her dancing became more fluid.

He twisted her around and wrapped one hand loosely around her waist, pulling her back against his chest. When her hips moved in a rhythmic, circular motion, he inhaled sharply. She let him grind on her soft ass, and he became as hard as granite, the arm around her tightening and pressing her closer.

"That's it." He murmured the encouragement while his heart raced in time to the percussive beat.

Her soft body moving against his weakened his willpower and doused his skin in flames. Curiosity overcame him. What would her lips taste like? He'd wondered ever since he saw her lick the beignet. Maybe before that, when he first saw her outside the SJ Brands building, on the sidewalk, staring at him.

With a hand under her chin, he tilted back her head and gazed down into her hooded eyes. She obviously felt it, too—this burning need to connect. Right then, he made a decision. He knew he shouldn't, knew what was at stake, but couldn't resist the need to kiss her any more than he could resist the need to breathe.

"Fuck it," he ground out.

He captured her mouth. There was no mere pop. No paltry zing. There was an explosion of sensation as heat engulfed him and he momentarily forgot that he was surrounded by moving bodies on the dance floor. He'd anticipated this moment for a long time, and the searing kiss spiked his blood and sent his pulse into overdrive. Time stood still as his mouth moved over hers.

She twisted in his arms, and her fingers fisted his shirt. Their contact deepened with an open-mouthed caress. He drank his fill, satiating the thirst for her kisses.

He kissed her deeper and harder, plunging his tongue into her mouth. One hand lowered and grabbed her right butt cheek. Hungry for more, he lifted his head, breaths coming in short, heavy bursts. Flames of desire licked at his loins.

He wanted all of her. Now. This minute.

"Let's get out of here," he said.

She nodded, gazing up at him with those expressive brown eyes and lips swollen from his kisses. No way had she heard him. His voice was much lower than the beat of the loud music, so she must have read his lips.

He clasped her hand in his and led the way out of the club.

CHAPTER 11

"*Y*ou smell so damn good," Stephan said in a gruff voice, standing before Roselle in only a pair of boxers, his eyes darkened to milk chocolate in color.

That's precisely the effect she'd wanted and why she'd rubbed almond-scented body butter into her skin after taking a quick shower. When they left Le Rêve, their make-out session had continued in the back of a taxi that took them through the streets of Paris to the apartment. Stephan had fondled her breasts and nibbled on her neck, at one point dragging her onto his lap and grinding against her core.

By the time the driver dropped them in front of the apartment building, her nipples had been so hard and the flesh between her legs so wet, she was ready to tear his clothes off. But she'd asked Stephan to let her take a shower first, and God bless him, he'd agreed, though he'd repeated the words *Take a shower?* in a confused voice, as if they were spoken in a language he didn't understand.

His warm hands spawned her waist under the nightshirt she wore, and he kissed her slowly, languidly, hungrily. Her nostrils were filled to the brim with the scent of him, a fresh pine scent, because he must have taken a shower, too.

With her pulse drumming a hard beat in her throat, Roselle slid the tip of her tongue to the seal of his lips and nudged them apart, giving him an enthusiastic French kiss. She sucked his tongue and moved hers within the interior of his mouth while his fingers inched below the waistband of her underwear and cupped her bottom.

Moaning softly, Roselle was overcome by all the pent-up desire suddenly allowed to break free. Her fingers roamed over his hard chest and encountered solid muscle.

His half-naked body didn't disappoint. He was exquisitely male, muscular without the bulk, with narrow hips and a lean waist. His long legs were toned and sprinkled with fine hairs that tickled her palms when she explored his sandy skin.

The kiss turned fiery, and Stephan's hands went to work. He squeezed her ass and pulled her onto her toes against the hard arousal in his boxers.

He quickly unbuttoned the nightshirt, tossed it aside, and lifted her onto the bed. Lying back on the pillows completely naked, she held her breath while his gaze hungrily assessed her breasts, as if he didn't know which one to start on first.

He massaged her breasts, lifting and squeezing them both before sucking a nipple into his mouth. The pad of his thumb raked over the other breast, and he squeezed it hard, forcing her to lift off the bed and moan at the pleasure his masterful touch inflicted.

Stephan kissed down the middle of her chest, moving swiftly toward his goal with single-minded determination, unleashing a horde of butterflies in her stomach.

By the time his tongue caressed her inner thighs, she was aching for him and ready to beg. She'd never known this feeling before. This unbearable throbbing. This unbearable wanting that threatened to consume her.

Stephan spread her legs, and the whisper of his breath kissed her damp flesh before he put his mouth to her. With a leisurely lick of his wide tongue, he dragged along her slit and made her grip the bedsheets. She very nearly fell apart at the intimate slide of his tongue along the heated flesh between her thighs.

He owned her sex, taking full possession of it with his mouth. Every time he stroked through the dewy wetness, she let out a soft, helpless cry. Toes tight, she rocked into his mouth, eyelids half-closed as she watched him between her thighs. She held out for as long as she could, but his skilled mouth, the sight of his muscular shoulders, and the soft groans he emitted as if he was loving every minute of his task were too much. The mounting pressure pushed free, and she cried out in ecstasy, her naked body arching toward the ceiling.

She tried to escape him, digging her heels into the mattress and scooting back on the bed, but Stephan held onto her thighs, his face still buried between her legs, focused on wringing every last tremor from her trembling body.

When he was finished, he crawled up on the bed with a satis-fied smirk on his face. "I knew your pussy would taste good," he said huskily.

He captured her mouth and weaved his tongue between her lips, forcing her to taste herself in his passionate kiss.

When he released her mouth and stepped off the bed and removed his boxers, his fully naked body didn't disappoint. She took inventory of every groove and sinewy muscle and his long, thick shaft, hard and ready to slide between her legs. Her legs fell apart, and his very aroused body settled between them. She ached to give him whatever he wanted, whatever he demanded.

The tip of her tongue grazed his ear, tracing the shell and generating a series of shudders along the length of his body. Her hands learned his shape, trailing over his skin, gliding up his ribcage and smoothing down his abdomen to follow the trail of hairs that ended between his legs and surrounded his sensitive flesh.

Emboldened, Roselle pushed Stephen onto his back and gave him the same sensual treatment he had given her. She nibbled on his hard pecs and sucked on his nipples. His groans were her reward, the inarticulate words he whispered as he gripped her neck were immensely satisfying and ego-stroking.

Kissing her way down his torso, she took pleasure in feeling him squirm under her mouth. Her teeth grated against his pelvis, and her tongue followed with a soothing caress.

She slid a hand over his impressive erection and took him in her mouth, tonguing his length and sucking hard until his arched throat corded with strain and his voice was a gravelly fragment of itself. His hand fastened on the ponytail at the back of her head and urged her to take him deeper. Guttural groans confirmed his pleasure as she let the tip hit the back of her throat. A series of curse words flew from his mouth, and she thought for sure that he was about to come.

But without warning, she was yanked up his body and compelled to lay on him as he caught his breath.

"I want to be inside you first," Stephan whispered, flipping her onto her back.

He picked up one of the condoms he'd placed on the bedside table when he first came into the room and put it over his erection. With a slide of his knee, he pried her legs apart and restrained her wrists on either side of her head. For a split second, she hesitated, an unrepressed memory burned into her brain, shooting forward to cause fear and confusion.

But she looked up into those whiskey-brown eyes and knew that she was safe, and her reservations fell away. This was Stephan. She let him in, eager and ready to explore this intimacy with him.

He advanced into her core with slow, deliberate movements and her body held onto him like the clasp of a satin glove.

"This must be what heaven feels like," he whispered.

She whimpered his name, begging him to continue. She wanted him to feed her on pleasure until she lost her mind. He absorbed her pleas with whispered words against her lips, his big body claiming and riding into hers.

His hands released her wrists and grasped her bottom. He spread her butt cheeks apart, intensifying the pleasurable sensations as he lifted her hips into the pump of his pelvis. He continued the erotic assault, thrusts coming harder and transforming into powerful drives that pushed them closer to climactic relief.

"I'm not satisfied until you're satisfied, sweetness," Stephan whispered.

He sucked on her neck and kicked off the tremors of a powerful orgasm that snaked through her body like a river on steroids. She clung to him, matching his frenzied motion, the strive to completion her whole focus now.

"Stephan," she cried out on the verge of tears, burying her face in his neck. Unraveling like a spool of thread, she breathed in the mixture of clean skin and sweat, clutching his head and pumping until she had no strength, nothing left but sensation.

With a final squeeze of her ass, he emptied into the condom and shuddered above her. Their bodies remained wrapped together for a long time until their heart rates lowered, and their breathing returned to normal.

* * *

STEPHAN WAS SO CONFIDENT, walking around naked, his sandy-gold skin on display in the light coming through the large uncovered windows. He had gone into the kitchen and brought back a bottle of water for each of them. He set hers on the table in case she became thirsty later, and guzzled half of his while standing beside the bed.

Roselle didn't know why, but she pulled the sheet up to her chin.

He arched an eyebrow, amusement gracing his features. "I've seen and touched everything."

She laughed, nestling against the fluffy pillows. "I know. I don't know why I'm doing this."

She would never look at his mouth or fingers the same ever

again. She'd always remember how he traced the lines of her body with each digit and his lips—*goodness*—the pleasure they evoked.

Stephan joined her in the bed and lay on his side, facing her. "Tired? Ready to go to sleep?"

Roselle shook her head.

"No? Then tell me what you want," he whispered.

"You. I want you again."

"Me, huh?" He traced the edge of her bottom lip with his finger. "Interesting, because I want you again, too."

Amazingly, after two orgasms, she still warmed to the thought of making love to him again. Stephan eased closer and kissed her lips.

"Every part of you is delicious," he said huskily.

She bit her lip, blushing, and he chuckled.

Taking her wrist, he rolled onto his back and pulled her on top of him. The heat of his growing erection warmed her inner thigh, and she rubbed her aching sex against it to alleviate the mushrooming throb of desire.

Overcoming her shyness, she kissed him fully—harder, greedier. He sucked on her chin and licked the underside of her neck, and when his hands slid beneath the sheet and cupped her butt cheeks, she was lost.

CHAPTER 12

"*B*race yourself. You are about to go on the greatest sightseeing tour of your life. It's going to be memorable. Epic," Stephan said, as they strolled to the metro station.

His clothes consisted simply of jeans and a tan, short-sleeved pullover, but on Stephan, they looked like designer wear. Roselle had brushed her hair into a sleek ponytail and was dressed in a pair of khaki capris, a white shirt, and flats.

"I appreciate the lack of hyperbole," she quipped.

"Smart ass." He swatted her on the behind, and she came to a full stop, staring at him with wide eyes.

"You can't do that."

"Why not? You let me do it last night," he said with a sly grin.

"That was different," she said in a low voice as if people were nearby listening to them, instead of going about their business.

Walking backward, Stephan said, "We have a lot of ground to cover today. Hurry up before we miss the train, woman."

She ran to catch up with him.

This morning they ate breakfast at a nearby cafe. He didn't say what she was thinking, that they shouldn't have had sex last night. They simply pretended that it was normal. Maybe for Paris, this was normal. She still felt him everywhere, all over. As if he were still on top of her and blanketing her skin.

Since Paris and its suburbs covered a large area, Stephan suggested they use the city's rapid transit system, saying it was an excellent way to sightsee and add another piece to the Paris experience, which Roselle happily agreed to.

They took the subway to the first stop, the Louvre, the world's largest art museum—so huge it would take months to see all the exhibits. Instead of going through the famous pyramid entrance and having to stand in the long line, Stephan took her through a lesser-known entrance, into an underground shopping mall where they were able to enter the museum within minutes. Using a map, they established a game plan and spent time browsing through Egyptian antiquities and Islamic art.

Then, of course, they had to stop at the Mona Lisa by Leonardo da Vinci. The iconic painting hung on a wall by itself, protected by bullet-proof glass. A crowd of tourists gazed up at it, many of them snapping photos and selfies to share with friends or social media followers.

"It's smaller than I expected," Roselle whispered.

"It's thirty inches by twenty-one inches. You want a photo?" Stephan whispered back.

She nodded and handed over her phone, then posed with one hand on her hip, head tilted to the side, and her best smile. She waited as Stephan stared at the screen, his expression unreadable. It was as if he'd forgotten to take the photo—forgotten she was standing there, though he was looking at her image.

"Are you going to take the picture or not?" she asked.

He glanced up as if she'd caught him off guard. "Calm down." He snapped several photos and then showed her the lot.

Roselle examined the pictures. She looked like a woman who didn't have a care in the world, and that's exactly how she felt at the moment.

"You like them?" Stephan asked.

"Yeah, I like them." A faint pulse of pain entered her chest. This happiness—this joy that she was experiencing, would probably end when they flew back to Atlanta.

"You want one?" she asked.

He shook his head. "I've been here before. I took photos standing in front of the Mona Lisa years ago."

They continued to browse the exhibits, but after a while, Roselle grew tired, and Stephan suggested they take a break and eat at a brasserie a couple of streets over from the usual tourist haunts. Outside, she took a photo at the Louvre's pyramid, and then they went to the eatery.

They lingered over wine and an omelet and salad for him, and a salade niçoise for her. He told her stories about his travels throughout France. How he and his siblings spent a month in Marseille one summer, soaking up the rays at the beach and then flitted off to their cousins' house in the south of France.

Roselle prodded him with questions, gasping from time to time, and downright ignoring her food in favor of giving him her rapt attention. His life was so fascinating and enriched because of his family, friends, and experiences. She missed having all of that but remained closed off, distancing herself as a coping mechanism and for her own self-preservation. She envied him and the valuable relationships he'd fostered over the years.

Energized by the meal and conversation, they were ready for the next stop, Stephan's favorite place in the city—Sacré-Cœur.

"What's so great about it?" she asked.

He flung an arm around her shoulders, and she melted into him, immensely comforted under his arm. Touching him had become as natural as seeing or walking.

"You'll see," he said.

They walked like that until they descended into the next station and took the subway to the Barbès neighborhood. As they left the station, Stephan waved off an Arab man who approached holding out a gold chain for the low, low price of fifteen euros.

"This is another side of Paris, the so-called 'immigrant neighborhood,'" he explained. "Mostly Arabs and Black people from former French colonies. It's where you'll get some of the best ethnic food. There's a place down there where you can get some delicious pho, and two streets over, the falafels will make you want to slap your momma."

Roselle giggled. "They're really that good?"

"Better."

They hurried across the street.

This part of Paris was definitely a melting pot, with a mix of cultures condensed into one place. On the way to their destination, they passed a man roasting corn on a grill, wig shops, and a halal butcher.

Stephan pointed out one of the souvenir stores. "This is a good place to get gifts. We can stop here on the way back."

She stuck close to him as they walked through the crowded streets. She noticed how men and women's eyes lingered on him. He stood out, and they probably were trying to figure out if he was someone famous. A model or a movie star, perhaps.

They walked up a sharp incline until they arrived at the bottom of the wide staircase that led to Sacré-Cœur, or the Sacred Heart Church, which opened in 1914. Constructed from white stone, the basilica stood out like a beacon on a hill, especially in the nighttime photos she'd seen online.

Instead of taking the funicular, they decided to climb the stairs. On the way up, they both dropped a few bills into the open guitar case of a musician strumming a tune at the bottom of the steps. The steps themselves were crowded with people chatting, drinking, and eating, which meant Stephan and Roselle had to weave their way up through the visitors.

At the very top, they went inside the church and viewed the elaborately designed interior, stained glass windows, as well as one of the largest ceiling mosaics in the world, depicting a risen Christ. When they exited, they stood atop the stairs where a panoramic view of the city was laid out before them, with landmarks like the Eiffel Tower and Montparnasse visible in the distance.

Roselle sighed with contentment. "I see why you like this spot."

They could see for miles and remained motionless for a while, absorbing the view in silence. Something about being here made her feel calm and free, alive.

She snapped some photos and then they were on their way again. They paused to watch a young man display his acrobatic skills with a soccer ball, much to the delight of the crowd who gasped and clapped as dusk settled over the city.

Their temporary stop ended up lasting almost an hour because other entertainers came through. Like any big city, there was no shortage of talented people to perform publicly for money. There was a male operatic singer and a juggler who wowed the crowd with precarious tricks as he hopped up and down the steps while catching and tossing bowling pins in the air.

Stephan glanced at the time. "We better go if we don't want to miss our ride on the Seine."

She anxiously agreed because the river cruise was on her must-do list. On the way back to the subway, they made a quick stop at the souvenir shop, and Roselle picked up an *I Love Paris* T-shirt for her great-aunt and a scarf with images of Paris landmarks all over it.

They arrived at the Bateaux Mouches pier on the Seine with two minutes to spare and hopped aboard the cruise with the other riders. They sailed past the Eiffel Tower, Notre Dame, and other tourist attractions before returning to the pier.

It was completely dark when the boat docked. Stephan glanced at his watch and asked, "Dinner first and then La Tour Eiffel?" he asked.

"Sounds good to me."

They ate a light dinner and then walked to Place du Trocadéro, a public square set on a hill across from the Eiffel Tower, so they could see the next time the tower lit up.

"This is where you want to take your pictures of La Tour Eiffel," Stephan said.

The gathered crowd included people hawking souvenirs, street performers, and tourists. Roselle waited anxiously, and right on time at ten o'clock, the twinkling lights lit up the massive structure from top to bottom, and everyone moaned and gasped in delight. She videotaped the event and took a video of herself, talking into the camera.

"I'm at the Eiffel Tower!" she exclaimed.

Five minutes later, the display was over.

"Did we get everything in?" Stephan asked.

"We did. You're a great guide." She couldn't have asked for a better escort to see Paris on her birthday.

Stephan frowned at her. "Hey, did you get any souvenirs for yourself?"

"I don't need anything. I have pictures, videos, and memories. More than anything, I wanted to see this landmark, and I have. I don't care about anything else."

"Hang on a sec," Stephan said and started walking away.

"Where are you going?" Roselle called after him.

"Don't move."

He disappeared into the crowd, and when he reappeared, he held up a tiny metal replica of the Eiffel Tower on a keychain.

"Happy birthday. Now you have a proper souvenir."

Roselle took the gift. It probably only cost him a few euros, but the thought behind the gift made her heart feel full.

"You can't help yourself, can you?" she asked.

"What do you mean?" Despite the lack of light, she saw the genuine confusion on his beautiful face.

"You're always doing for other people."

"I just thought you'd like it."

Roselle raised up on tiptoe and kissed his cheek. "No matter what you like to pretend, you're a sweetheart, Stephan. Thank you."

"I guess it takes one to know one," he said quietly.

She only smiled, and then they left the site.

CHAPTER 13

"*T*here's one more thing we have to do," Stephan said.

"What else do you have planned?"

"Do you like surprises?"

"No," Roselle said with a little laugh, though she was starting to, thanks to him.

"Pretend you do for now. I need to take you to a spot near the apartment. It's a bakery, and I want you to meet the owner."

"Why?"

"Don't worry about that," he said enigmatically.

He hailed a taxi, and they climbed in and headed back to the seventh arrondissement. Roselle stared out at the people and the cars going by, her heart turning as heavy as a block of stone. She already missed this place. The lights, the energy, the food, and the sights. She should have asked for more time. Two days wasn't enough.

They pulled up outside a bakery, and after paying, Stephan exited the vehicle. He gave Roselle a helping hand.

"It's closed," she remarked. The display window was dark, and a single light above the door cast light on the doorstep.

"Closed to the public, but not to us. I know the owner, and he's cool." Stephan walked confidently up to the glass door and knocked.

"Are you sure? I feel awful disturbing him like this." She still didn't know why they were there, but it had something to do with her, which made her feel worse.

"Don't. He lives upstairs and doesn't mind. He's in love with my mother and would do anything for her, and by extension, anything for me. Trust me, it's not a big deal."

After a few minutes, a light came on in the back, and a dark form shuffled toward them. A portly older man opened the door, and the wrinkles in his face ironed out as his face brightened into a smile.

"*Bonsoir*, Henri."

"Stephan, *bonsoir*! It has been a long time. Good to see you. *Comment ça va?*" He and Stephan kissed once on each cheek.

"I'm doing well. I'm here on business for my mother."

Henri pressed a hand to his heart. "Ah, Sylvie. How is she, my love, my heart?"

Stephan let out a laugh. "You had your chance and didn't make a move. Now she and my father are back together."

Henri looked crestfallen. "I know. I only hope he makes a mistake, and she will soon be free again. Next time, I will not miss my chance!" He looked at Roselle.

Stephan spoke up immediately. "This is Roselle."

"*Enchanté.*" Henri kissed her on each cheek. "Welcome. Stephan told me it is your birthday. Happy birthday to you."

"Thank you," she said.

"Come in." Henri ushered them into the bakery and locked the door.

"Do you have everything ready?" Stephan asked.

"*Mais oui. Asseyez-vous.*" He motioned to a table set with two chairs in front of the window. Then he disappeared.

"What are you up to?" Roselle whispered.

"Have. A. Seat." Stephan kept an enigmatic expression on his face. He pulled out a chair.

Roselle glared at him, but deep down, she was excited. The trip so far had been fantastic, so what had he arranged? She sat in the chair, and then the thought came to her. They were in a bakery. Did he get her a cake? If taste was determined by smell alone, this bakery was a winner. From the moment they entered, her nostrils had been filled with the enticing scent of breads and pastries.

Stephan sat down across from her. "Honestly, it's not that big of a deal. I wanted to do a little something for you."

Her stomach tightened. He was so handsome, so magnificently male with his square jaw and a tight body she'd enjoyed exploring last night. And surprisingly kind—kinder than expected.

She wished to prolong their time together, to bask in the energy and vibrance of his charismatic personality. Before him, her life had been dull and boring. In less than forty-eight hours, he'd forced her to see the technicolor world that surrounded her and embrace excitement instead of shunning it.

Roselle leaned over the table and whispered, "Did Henri stand a chance with your mother?"

Stephan shook his head. "My mother has a height requirement. She wants a man who's taller than her when she's in heels. My father barely made the cut."

Roselle laughed. "I met your dad once. They seem very, um…" She searched for the right word, worried she'd offend.

"Different? Like polar opposites?" Stephan supplied.

"Yes."

"That's because they are. My mother's high-strung and my father keeps her calm. At the same time, being with her excites him. I'm sure his life was boring as hell without her."

"Funny how some people gravitate toward each other."

"People you don't expect to work as a couple. Sometimes you have no idea what you're missing until you're staring right at it. Some people need to be grounded. Calmed down."

Roselle nodded. "Others need to live their lives and have fun for a change."

Their gazes met across the table as thunder softly grumbled a warning.

As longing stuck in her throat, Roselle glanced out at the street. A car passed by slowly, and a woman on a bike rolled by with a baguette sticking out of a tote on the back. She didn't want to leave because everything would change when they returned to the U.S.

Henri approached with a tray. On top of it were three lit candles in the middle of a chocolate torte.

Roselle's mouth fell open. Across the table, Stephan wore a smug, satisfied expression on his face.

"Happy birthday." Henri set the cake in the middle of the round table, along with a knife, two plates, and forks.

"*Merci*," Stephan said.

"*Merci*," Roselle said.

"*De rien*, and take all the time you need."

When he was gone, Roselle stared at the cake.

"Make a wish," Stephan said.

"I don't know what to say. Why did you do this?" she asked in a thick voice.

Stephan folded his arms on the table. "Because I wanted to. Make a wish."

Tears blurred her vision, and Roselle closed her eyes to keep him from seeing.

She almost wished this night would never end, but that was silly. The night would be over soon, and then she'd go back to the reality of Atlanta. Work. The quiet aloneness of her apartment. Unless Stephan wanted more than a hookup. Did he?

She opened her eyes, and he was staring at her.

There was very little light inside the bakery. The street lights provided a glow, and the light in the back also provided illumination, while the candlelight flickered across his smooth, sandy-gold skin.

"Did you make your wish?" he asked.

I wish you were mine.

"Yes," she answered and blew out the candles.

Stephan did the honor of cutting the cake, and they both indulged in huge slices of chocolate on chocolate that rivaled any dessert she'd ever had before. At the very least, it was the best chocolate cake she'd ever had.

After they'd cleaned their plates, Stephan called out to Henri, and the baker came back to the front.

"This is for your mother," he said, handing Stephan a paper sack.

"Macaroons?" Stephan asked.

"Yes. Tell her they're from the man who still loves her and waits until she is free again."

Stephan chuckled. "My father might kill me, but I'll relay the message. Thanks for tonight. You made my friend's birthday very special."

"*Merci beaucoup*, Henri. The cake was delicious," Roselle said.

"It was my pleasure." Thunder rolled again, and Henri stared out the window with a frown. "You must hurry before the rain comes. One moment, before you go." He went behind the counter and came back with a white box. "You will take this with you and enjoy the rest later." He boxed up the cake and then handed it to Roselle with a flourish.

She gave him a quick hug, and then they were on their way.

Roselle waved at him one last time as she went out the door. "Thanks again."

"*Bon voyage!*" He waved at them from the threshold and then closed the door.

They set out on foot since the apartment was nearby.

"What am I supposed to do with this?" She held up the box as if Stephan didn't know she had it.

"Eat it," he quipped.

"I can't eat this much cake, though I am tempted." She gave him a sidelong glance. "You're not so bad, Stephan."

He laughed. "I'm terrible, but sometimes I get it right."

She was starting to wonder if his whole persona was a front. He clearly had a big heart, and he was thoughtful and considerate.

The fact that he slept around and had had several brushes with the law was definitely a negative, but he had redeeming qualities. He certainly was not what she expected when he started working at SJ Brands.

"What are you going to miss most about Paris?" Stephan asked as they walked along the cobblestoned street.

"Everything."

"Come on, you have to be specific."

I'll miss spending time with you.

"No, really. Everything. I love the food, I love the old buildings, I love hearing people talk with a French accent, and I like moments like this…walking along the street with cars going by and people strolling past. I feel like I'm in another world."

"It is a very unique place," Stephan agreed.

A drop of water plopped onto Roselle's nose. She wiped it away and looked up. More drops fell from the sky.

"Uh-oh, there's that rain we suspected was coming."

The drops fell heavier.

"Come on, we're almost there." Stephan grabbed the hand not holding the cake box, and they took off running.

Roselle lifted her eyes skyward and laughed. She was in Paris, running through the streets in the rain, on her birthday, with a handsome man by her side. They arrived at the doorway of the apartment building without getting completely soaked, though her hair and clothes were damp. They sheltered on the stoop, heaving and out of breath.

Roselle stared up at the stormy sky. "The perfect ending to the best birthday ever."

When her eyes shifted to Stephan, he was staring at her with an intensity that made her heart constrict.

"Glad I was a part of it." His chest rose and fell with the same frequency as hers.

She swallowed against the lump burgeoning in her throat. "You were the best part of it. Because of you, I'll never forget today and tonight. Thank you."

Time stood still as the rain fell around them. Then Stephan stepped slowly toward her, and she didn't move, remaining locked in place. The air between them noticeably shifted.

He took her chin and tilted her head up to his. "I keep thinking about last night."

"Me too," she whispered.

A muscle in his jaw clenched, and with a low groan, he pushed her against the cement and pressed his lips into hers. He didn't use his tongue. His soft lips hit up against hers over and over again, plucking, teasing, and torturing with a caress that was sensual and intimate.

Much as she'd enjoyed the cake, she wished she didn't have it in her hand at the moment because it kept her from fully embracing him. Head tilted back, she pressed into him, using her free hand to cup his jaw and savor the sweetness of his chocolate-flavored mouth as he deepened the kiss. Stephan finally sucked in her tongue. She let out a soft moan and shivered against him. His head lowered as he kissed the side of her neck, licking away the water and setting her skin on fire.

"Stephan," she whispered, her voice a weak fraction of itself.

"Let's take this inside," he said in a husky voice.

She nodded her assent. She didn't care about anything else right now except getting him between her legs.

His hand slid down and squeezed her bottom, long fingers gripping the flesh, possessively kneading and exploring her ass. He kissed her neck and turned her toward the door. Roselle thought he was about to grind against her ass, but instead, he entered the code.

His hand remained on her bottom, and she wondered if he'd forgotten it there. But it seemed to belong, part of her now, the casual hold on her body heightening her awareness of the sexual energy between them and making her wet panties wetter.

Once inside, his hand shifted higher to the small of her back, and he guided her to the elevator. They rode up to the apartment in silence and once inside, placed their items in the refrigerator.

Standing so close behind her that his warm body heated hers, Stephan didn't waste any time. He kissed her neck and cupped her breasts from behind. Roselle groaned softly and let him guide her to his bedroom.

The subtle smell of him filled the room—the scent of his cologne, the scent of his maleness.

"This is our last night in Paris," she whispered with a heavy heart.

"Then let's make it count."

They stripped out of their clothes and climbed into the bed. Nipples tight, breasts heavy and aching, Roselle welcomed him into her open arms. His mouth crashed onto hers, his hard length grinding into the wetness between her legs. Their bodies meshed together almost immediately, with urgency. He groaned as she licked his Adam's apple and grabbed his tight ass.

His pistoning hips filled her with his length, racing them both toward the ultimate goal. In no time at all, she was screaming, clutching his ass cheeks, tossing her head back as a blindingly magnificent orgasm launched her into the stratosphere.

Later—much, much later—when the rain had stopped, and they were both exhausted from another bout of lovemaking, she was gently brought awake by a light flitting across her eyelids.

She and Stephan lay with their heads on the same pillow, his arm thrown across her waist from behind, his soft breaths brushing the back of her neck. And outside, the lights of the Eiffel Tower twinkled against the backdrop of the dark night sky.

CHAPTER 14

They agreed not to tell anyone. Not about last night or the
night before.

But that didn't stop the ache of disappointment when Roselle
woke up alone in bed. After sharing another night with Stephan,
she'd hoped to find his warm body next to hers. Swallowing back
her disappointment, she rolled off the mattress and dressed in last
night's discarded clothes.

She exited the room and peeped out the door. No sign of
Stephan, but she heard him and Giles talking in the kitchen. She
scurried up the stairs and went into the bathroom to prepare for
the day.

After a shower, she donned a solid purple maxi-dress with
short sleeves for the long flight home. She combed her hair away
from her face and took a deep breath.

She could do this, right? He had a great time. She had a great
time. It was only casual sex—no commitment, no emotions,
precisely what she'd expected.

As she descended the stairs, the smell of coffee and breakfast
fixings greeted her nose. She walked through the living room into
the dining area and swallowed hard when she saw Stephan at the
table, sipping coffee and staring at his phone. He wore jeans and a

red T-shirt that said *Naughty by Nature* in white letters. When she approached, he glanced up.

"Good morning," she said cheerily.

He frowned for a split second and then it was gone. "Good morning," he said, his face impassive. His gaze scoured her ensemble and heated her skin.

Giles appeared from the kitchen. "*Bonjour, mademoiselle.* What can I get you to eat? An American breakfast or a French breakfast?"

"What's the difference?" Roselle sat across from Stephan.

"American, I can make a full meal as I did for Stephan, with eggs, bacon or sausage—or both. If you'd like pancakes or toast, I can prepare that, too. Whatever you like. French breakfast is much simpler. You have a choice of *pain au chocolat*, a croissant, or bread and jam." Giles folded his hands in front of him and waited for her decision.

"I'll take an American breakfast—eggs, sunny-side up, sausage, and I'll have a croissant with jam, please."

"*Bon.* Coffee?"

"Yes. Black."

Roselle sat quietly, pretending to be preoccupied with the contents of the table for the seconds that it took Giles to go into the kitchen and bring out a white carafe of coffee. He flipped over her mug and filled it three-quarters of the way. The entire time, Stephan didn't say a word, but she felt his eyes on her.

When Giles went back into the kitchen, Stephan spoke. "You have plans when you get back?" he asked.

Before answering the question, Roselle sipped her coffee and hoped he didn't notice the slight tremor in her hand. Why was she always so unbalanced around him?

"I'll probably go straight home to take a nap and then visit my aunt tomorrow to give her the souvenirs and share pictures of the trip. You?"

"Probably do the same thing—go home and take a nap. After that, who knows?"

He bent his head over the phone again, and Roselle sipped her coffee. She wanted to yell and scream at him. Did their time together in Paris mean nothing? Did the two nights they spent together mean nothing? Did he really intend for them to act as if nothing happened? She could have been Namia for all he seemed to care.

A man like him was used to having one-night stands, and she'd have to adjust to fit within whatever guidelines he was accustomed to, act as detached as he did. The last thing he'd want was for her to be clingy, and that's the last thing she wanted, too.

But that didn't stop the pain in her heart from spilling into her chest, making it hurt with unexpected ferocity as if someone had continuously punched her in the same spot without reprieve.

Giles brought a plate with her breakfast choices. "Thank you," she murmured.

A few minutes later, Stephan dismissed Giles. The butler set the carafe of coffee on the table and exited the apartment.

While Stephan scrolled through whatever he was looking at on his phone, she was consumed by insecurities. What did he think of her?

"Do you think I'm a slut?" Roselle blurted.

Stephan's head shot up, and he stared at her with his mouth dropped open. "What? No. Why'd you ask me some shit like that?"

She'd been called that before. As the sunlight came in through the windows, its brightness shined on memories so ugly she couldn't face them.

She set down her fork. "Nothing. I'm being ridiculous."

"You asked me for a reason. Why? Because we slept together?"

She let out a shaky breath. "Yes," she admitted quietly, staring at her plate of food.

"Sweetheart, we slept *together*. If you're a slut, then I'm a slut, too. And I'm no slut."

She looked at him and saw no trace of condemnation, which gave her relief. The negative thoughts would have tormented her indefinitely if she hadn't asked. She would have second-guessed her actions, and despite his behavior now, the last two nights had been magical. She didn't want to regret what she'd done. Not like she had all those nights ago.

"Good. I should have known you were different."

She was about to dive back into her plate when he said her name. She looked up and saw concern etched his features.

He rubbed a hand over the back of his head. "Listen, the last two nights have been great, and—"

"You don't have to say another word," Roselle interjected, keeping her voice light and playful. She added an amused expression, hoping her eyes didn't expose the burden of pain in her heart.

She didn't need a speech. She couldn't bear to hear him diminish what they'd shared, so she spoke up to lessen the pain and humiliation. To prove they were on the same page.

"I have absolutely no expectations. We had fun, we had great sex. You made my birthday memorable, that's for sure. Obviously, we can't continue screwing around when we get back to Atlanta. I mean, we work together, and that would be a disaster." She added a laugh for good measure. "But we'll always have Paris, and what more could a girl ask for?"

She dropped her gaze and sliced a sausage link in two. She ate one half, barely tasting the meat because her senses were numb.

Stephan pushed back his chair and stood, towering over the table. "I need to finish packing. Sébastien will be here in thirty minutes to take us to the airport." His eyes were guarded.

"I'll be ready." She put on a bright smile to hide the twist of pain her stomach.

His jawline hardened, and without another word, he left the table.

Roselle watched him walk across the living room floor until he disappeared behind the stairs. Having lost her appetite, she scooted the plate out of the way.

Why did these memories have to come back now? She pressed trembling fingers to her temple and closed her eyes, praying for the strength to shove back the painful thoughts that had pushed through when she opened her mind's door a crack.

At sixteen, she'd snuck out of the house to meet her friends at the local burger joint where fellow high-schoolers and college students hung out. When she arrived, her two girlfriends were crowded into a booth with three guys, one of them being Charles Baker, who'd recently graduated. She'd had a crush on him for years.

He was a basketball hero in their town, leading the varsity team to three state championships and taking home the trophy from one of them. With a basketball scholarship to Duke, everyone expected great things from him. He was good-looking and well over six feet, with sandy brown skin and a smile that could shame the sun into hiding.

Her girlfriends each left with their dates, and she was left with Charles. When he invited her for a ride in his graduation gift—a red Mustang—she became excited. But Charles Baker was a bad person. Later, she learned how bad he could be.

She should have known not to get into the car. She should have known not to go into the house because his parents were away for the weekend. She should have known not to go to his room when he coaxed her up there to look at his artwork, claiming they had something in common.

More than anything, she should have known that when he closed the door, he was not going to let her out, no matter how much she begged.

She had been called so many names. *Slut. Liar. Stupid. Gold-digger. Whore. Easy.* To this day she regretted her actions from that night. She didn't understand but accepted the doubts from the strangers, people who didn't know her. The real pain came because people she knew didn't stand by her.

The door to Stephan's bedroom opened, and she slammed the lid on the thoughts that would torment her if she let them. He set his suitcase at the front and then went back into his room.

The truth became as clear as black ink on a white sheet. She'd developed feelings for him in a short period—feelings she'd have to suffocate if she were going to be able to function at work.

She'd spent two days and two nights in Paris with a man who made her feel more like herself than she had in a long time. She'd become so settled in her routines over the years, but these past couple of days had reminded her that she was young and should have fun. Moving forward, she'd venture out more and join her roommate when she invited her to events. There was a whole world out there for her to explore and become a part of.

She couldn't have Stephan. But she could have Roselle back.

CHAPTER 15

"*Y*ou must have had a good time. You're smiling a lot and generally seem happy." Seated behind her desk, Sylvie fixed her eyes on Roselle. She looked very much the businesswoman in a white collared shirt, open at the top to show a string of pearls around her neck.

"We were in Paris, Mother. Of course, she enjoyed herself," Stephan said.

It was Monday morning, and he and Roselle sat across from Sylvie in her office, briefing her on the meetings with the Rue de la Mode reps, but he had a feeling his mother was fishing and wanted to cut off her investigation before Roselle said anything incriminating.

Sylvie's gaze shifted to Stephan, and she straightened the glasses on her nose. "I believe Roselle can speak for herself." She returned her attention to Roselle. "How was the nonbusiness part of the trip?"

"Excellent. I saw a lot of tourist attractions and filled up on delicious food," Roselle answered.

"I see. Well, I'm glad you enjoyed yourself."

Roselle shifted in the chair and crossed her legs.

Stephan's skin prickled at the sight of her bare knee, calves, and ankles—cinnamon-brown body parts his hands and mouth had become intimately familiar with over the course of two nights.

"Paris was truly amazing. I'd love to go back when I have more time," Roselle said.

Why was she smiling so much? What the hell did she have to be so goddamn happy about?

He'd been in a foul mood all weekend, thinking about their last conversation at the breakfast table and how she'd more or less blown off their time together. Granted, he hadn't expected them to have a relationship, and he'd prepared a speech where he'd let her know that what happened in Paris had to stay in Paris.

But then she'd hijacked the conversation and spoken so casually about their time together, he'd not only been thrown off guard, he'd been pissed. He was still pissed. They'd spent a lot of time together, and it meant nothing to her?

"My son took good care of you?" Sylvie asked.

"Yes, he did."

Roselle's voice had gone a little softer and made the hairs on the back of his neck stand up. Sylvie didn't seem to notice the change in her voice, but he sure did. It reminded him of their last night together.

With his back against the headboard, she sank onto his hard shaft reverse-cowgirl style, nestling her bottom onto his pelvis. Back arched, head thrown back so her eyes looked up at the ceiling, she'd ridden him hard. Her whispers of pleasure still echoed in his ears as she moaned about how much she enjoyed it, how she never wanted him to stop. Then she panted, "Oh, oh," as she came.

"What other information do you have for me?" Sylvie asked.

"Their stores are pristine, and in great locations. Management and staff are very knowledgeable, and we observed a lot of hand-selling with their customers," Roselle said.

"Sounds like you think we should work with them," Sylvie said

"They would be a good partner," Roselle said with confidence.

"What about you, Stephan? I know you're new at this, but what was your impression?"

Stephan repositioned in the chair, hoping his semi-erect penis didn't get any harder. "I feel the same as Roselle. I got a good feeling from them. They're very professional, too. No negatives that I saw."

"In that case, I'll relay your thoughts to Marcus, and we'll get business development and the legal department involved to start working on a deal. Thank you both."

Roselle and Stephan rose from their chairs and walked out of Sylvie's office. They passed through the reception area, giving a brief greeting to her assistant, before entering the elevator.

They rode down in silence, standing a few feet away from each other.

He smelled her perfume and wanted to reach for her. Wanted to press his nose to her neck and indulge in the fragrance in full.

"My mother seemed pleased," he said.

"Yes, I agree."

When the doors opened on their floor, she went left without another word. Shoving his hands in his pockets, Stephan gritted his teeth and headed back to his office, determined to get Roselle Parker out of his mind.

* * *

He was staring at her.

Stephan's gaze burned her skin from the other side of the table. She wrote an unnecessary note on a page of her legal pad, hoping she appeared nonchalant. If he continued to look at her like that, everyone would guess what they'd done in Paris—and that she wanted to do it again. And again. And again.

"That's all for now. We can reconvene in another month once we've had a chance to talk to legal," said Marcus, the VP of business development. He was an older Black man, with a barrel-sized torso and his thick Afro and circle beard dotted with gray hairs.

A low murmur went up from the group as they stood and gathered up their tablets and pads. Roselle avoided eye contact with Stephan and walked out of the room alongside Jayson, who worked in business development. Their department was separated into geographic locations, and Jayson covered Canada and the United States, while Stephan learned as much as possible about all the territories.

Jayson was a good-looking guy about her age, with a goatee and friendliness that appeared anxious at times.

"Dress for the job you want and not the job you have," he'd told her once, and every day he wore a suit and tie. He aspired to be the next VP of business development when Marcus retired, but with Stephan working in that department now, his chance of taking over the role had probably taken a nose dive.

Ever since she'd come back from Paris, he'd been friendlier, and he'd asked a bunch of questions about her trip. She kept to the basics, only telling him about the meetings on the first day and her sightseeing on the second day. She excluded how she'd partied with Stephan and spent two nights in his arms.

"You have lunch plans?" Jayson asked in a low tone as they walked down the hall.

Roselle glanced at him. This was the second time he'd asked her about lunch. The first time he'd caught her coming back from Subway and said if he'd known she was eating alone, he would have joined her.

Stephan had seen them coming in as he was leaving out, and she'd glimpsed a healthy dose of disapproval in his face. She'd sent him a text right afterward, feeling like she needed to explain herself, though nothing was going on between her and Stephan or her and Jayson.

Roselle: *Jayson and I didn't have lunch together.*

Stephan: *Ur a free woman. U can do whatever you want.*

The dismissive response had been disappointing. Heart crushing.

"I'm eating lunch at my desk," she told Jayson.

"Too bad. Maybe another time?"

"Um, maybe."

She needed to be more direct, but she didn't want to hurt his feelings.

She went down the hall to the break room. Marcus was long-winded, so the meeting had gone over an hour when it should have lasted only thirty minutes. She hadn't had the forethought to take in a drink and was dying of thirst. She set her pad and pen on one of the round tables in the room, got a paper cup, and went over to the water dispenser.

She sensed the moment she was no longer alone, and though he didn't utter a word, she knew the person who'd entered was Stephan. His walk was distinctive. No one else moved like him.

Roselle turned around to face him. Today he wore a powder-blue shirt and dark slacks. Casually dressy, but the way he emanated power, he might as well have been wearing a three-piece Brioni suit.

"You have a new friend, I see," he remarked.

His face was impassive, so she had no idea what he was thinking. Like his mother, he was a master at hiding his emotions.

"Who?" she asked, feigning ignorance.

"Your boy, Jayson. You two seem mighty close all of a sudden."

She shrugged. "So?"

Why was he questioning her? He'd made it plain that she was free to do as she wanted, and though Jayson held no interest for her, perhaps she'd find someone else besides Stephan to occupy her thoughts.

She'd gone out with her roommate for the first time last weekend. A surgeon and his partner who lived in Grant Park had thrown a house party. Most of the guests worked in the medical field, and one of them—a doctor—had taken a particular interest in her. After she'd relaxed, he kept her attention with stories about the antics of some of his patients.

"The two of you seem kind of cozy, that's all," Stephan remarked.

Roselle turned away from him and poured water into the cup. "What do you care?" she asked.

"Oh, we're playing games now?"

She swung around in surprise. "I'm not playing games. I texted you, and you let me know that you don't care what I do."

"That's not what I said."

"But that's what you meant, so I'm confused as to why you're so interested in what Jayson and I are up to."

"So you're up to something?" he asked swiftly as if he'd caught her in a lie.

What was happening?

"That's my business." Roselle strode past him, but he grabbed her arm and water sloshed over her hand and onto the floor.

"Be careful with that guy."

"Why?"

"Something about him bugs me."

"He's a nice guy."

"He's trying too hard with his overly-friendly schtick."

"You wanted to be my friend at one time, remember? Since when is being friendly a problem?"

"Since he's being friendly with you."

"Now you're the one playing games." Roselle tugged her arm away, but the sensation of his touch remained as vivid as if he continued to hold her. "You're one of *those* guys. I don't want you, but I don't want anyone else to have you. Well, guess what? We both agreed to the rules, and we both have to stick to them. Please don't bother me again about who's being friendly with me. Leave me alone, and I'll leave you alone."

Roselle took up her pen and notepad and stalked out, immensely satisfied by the angry expression on Stephan's face. She was not going to be jerked around by him or anyone else. If he thought she'd be falling all over him like the girls in his Instagram photos, he had another think coming.

CHAPTER 16

 ith a grunt of disgust, Stephan shoved the document away that Marcus had given him to read. He'd reread the same paragraph three times and didn't comprehend the words any more than he did during the first read.

He thought about Paris all the time, or more specifically, Roselle. They'd returned from the trip over two weeks ago, and every time he saw her, he ached to touch her or bury his face in her scented neck. The urge to do so made his stomach hurt, as if a hole had opened in his gut, one that he couldn't close with any other woman because he didn't want another woman. He only wanted her.

And he didn't want anyone near her. That was his other problem. He definitely wasn't handling his jealousy well. One day when he was leaving out, he saw her coming into the building with Jayson. It was around lunchtime, so he assumed they'd had lunch together and the thought filled him with seething envy.

She was laughing so hard, he'd been a bit taken aback because he'd thought that expression had been reserved only for him. His ego had been crushed, thinking that maybe he wasn't that special.

As usual, Jayson had been particularly annoying. Since Stephan started working there, Jayson had constantly been in his face, being way too friendly. If he wasn't overly cheerful in the halls, he'd stop by Stephan's office and spend a few minutes talking about nothing in particular and including the occasional crass joke. Stephan's lack of enthusiasm didn't deter him, either. He reminded Stephan of a certain kind of person he sometimes encountered who was eager to please and thought the way to do it was by getting close to those in power and making inappropriate comments. There was no doubt in his mind that Jayson thought becoming friends with Sylvie Johnson's son was the right move.

When he saw Jayson and Roselle coming in from lunch, he'd had an unsettling urge to punch the guy, and all he'd done was greet Stephan with a smile.

Then there was the text she sent explaining about Jayson, and he'd sent a dickish response he now regretted. In all honesty, his feelings for Roselle was detrimental to his sanity. It was an obsessive compulsion to hold and guard and keep. He'd never been so possessive about a woman before. It was unhealthy, but he couldn't rein in his out-of-control emotions.

Two days and two nights. That's all it was. So why couldn't he let it go?

Stephan pushed away from the desk and looked around the boring office. His mother was really making him earn his keep. Most of the staff had painted their walls in some form or fashion—either all four walls or adding an accent wall. Sylvie had informed him that he could not paint the walls or get new furniture since she didn't know if he was staying. He had to spend every day in a boringly monochromatic office with white walls and slate gray furniture.

He stood, stretched, and then left the office. He needed to get out of the building. It was after five on a Friday, and he wouldn't get any more work done. Maybe he'd make some phone calls to invite over female company this weekend to take his mind off Roselle.

First, he'd get a soda in the break room and then head out.

When he stepped into the break room, who should he see but annoying old Jayson, standing at the drinks machine. He almost backed out of the room, but Jayson turned around and saw him.

"Hey man, what's up?"

"Hey." Stephan greeted him less enthusiastically.

"You go ahead. I don't know what I want yet." Jayson stepped aside.

Stephan walked up to the machine and reviewed the options.

"So... you and Roselle, are you...?"

His shoulders tensed. "Are we what?"

"Are you hitting that?"

Stephan's entire body stiffened. He'd bragged about his sexual exploits before, but never to someone who was essentially a stranger and he didn't like that the conversation was about Roselle.

He slowly turned around and faced Jayson. "What did you say?"

"You hitting that? Because she's a tough nut to crack. I've been trying to talk to her since she came back from Paris. I don't know what it is, but she seems different, but she won't accept any of my invitations to lunch, and she said she doesn't have a man. I figured she must be hooking up with somebody, and before the trip to Paris, I know you guys were having lunch together."

Stephan really couldn't believe this guy's audacity. One, for him to question him about Roselle, and two, his inability to read the temperature in the room. He quickly assessed Jayson, sizing him up and figuring out that he would be easy to intimidate. He wasn't quite six feet tall, and while he had a muscular body, he was smaller than Stephan.

"So because she won't give you the time of day, there must be someone else, and you assume that's me."

Jayson appeared uncertain all of a sudden, no longer wearing a sly, knowing grin.

"Listen, man, if I read the situation wrong—"

"Yeah, you read the situation all wrong."

"Guess I'll still shoot my shot then." Jayson laughed. "Between you and me, I like the quiet ones. They're the ones who surprise you in bed, you know? I bet Roselle is full of surprises." The sly grin came back, and he nudged Stephan with an elbow to solicit agreement, but that was the last straw.

Stephan was irritable, cranky, and in a bad mood in general. The last thing he wanted was to deal with this guy and his offensive comments. He shoved Jayson against the wall and gripped the lapels of his suit jacket. Jayson's eyes widened as Stephan brought his face within inches of his.

He spoke in a low, lethal voice. "I'm not your buddy, I'm not your man, I'm not your partner, so stop talking to me like we're friends. And definitely don't talk to me about Roselle Parker ever again. Matter of fact, stay away from her. She's too good for you."

He released Jayson and stalked out. Then he remembered he never purchased the drink he went in there for. He turned around and went back in. Jayson remained against the wall, his brow furrowed as if he were confused about what had taken place.

Stephan glared at him, and he straightened up, eyeing Stephan warily as he went to the machine. He slid a bill into the machine's slot and punched the soda he wanted. He glared at Jayson one more time for good measure and walked out.

Still fuming, he rode the elevator to the first floor and left the building. On the sidewalk, he came to a complete stop and forced pedestrians to go around him.

Speak of the devil.

Roselle was rushing toward the bus. Earlier she wore a pair of burgundy slacks and a cream-colored blouse. Now she wore high heels and a tight-fitting skirt that showed off the curves of her slim hips and cupped the shape of her butt. He was jealous of that skirt because it had permission to hold and mold against her body.

Damn, she looked sexy.

Why had she changed, and where was she going?

She climbed into the bus, and he watched it drive away.

Suddenly, the idea of calling another woman for company didn't hold the same appeal.

Roselle had his mind all messed up. Wherever she was going, that's where he wanted to be.

CHAPTER 17

*R*oselle marched into Stephan's office and slammed the door. She winced. She hadn't meant to close it that hard.

Stephan, standing over at the credenza, swung around from his task of rummaging through some pages. He scowled at her. "Nice entrance."

Roselle squared her shoulders and dived deep into the tough girl act she'd perfected. "We need to talk."

"About what?"

"About Jayson. Did you warn him away from me?"

Stephan snorted. "He told you? Punk." He turned back to the credenza and resumed flipping through the stack of papers.

"Excuse me, but this is important. Can I have your attention, please?"

Stephan turned to face her with eyebrows raised. "I'm sorry, Madame Parker. Please, continue."

He rested his butt against the edge of the credenza, folded his arms over his chest, and crossed his legs at the ankles. He looked relaxed and at ease, but he also appeared rather sexy with the muscles under his shirt bunching and hinting at the tightness of his body

Roselle almost forgot why she came in there.

"I'd appreciate it if you don't warn anyone away from me. First of all, it's inappropriate. Second of all, I can handle Jayson. If I wanted to get rid of him, I know how."

"So you want his attention?" Stephan asked sarcastically.

"No, I don't, but I also don't see the need to be rude."

"So I did you a favor. You should be thanking me."

"Really, Stephan?"

"What do you want me to say? That I'm sorry? Well, I'm not. Remember how you acted with Namia at Le Rêve? How you defended me? I did the same for you. You're welcome."

"I didn't act like a dog over a bone, and I wasn't rude to her."

"You sure about that?"

She reviewed the memory. Maybe she'd been a *little* rude when she stepped up. Definitely possessive. Okay, maybe a little bit like a dog over a bone.

"You know what, none of that matters. This is a place of business, and we have to conduct ourselves professionally. I don't want any trouble."

"Place of business or not, I don't like that guy, and I definitely don't like him sniffing around what belongs to me."

She stared at him in disbelief. "Belongs...*excuse you*? Nothing on me belongs to you."

"That pussy belongs to me."

"No, it does not!" she said hotly.

"You sure about that?" He tilted his head, gaze dragging over her in a possessive way. Then his eyes met hers head-on. "As far as I'm concerned, I licked it, so it's mine."

Heat flooded her cheeks, and Roselle took in a sharp breath, the memory of what he'd done surging back with unexpected intensity. He'd lapped at her like melting ice cream on a cone and made her scream with his insatiable appetite to satisfy.

"You say anything, don't you? You are so crude and so disgusting—"

Stephan slow-clapped as he pushed off the credenza, shaking his head in admiration. "Brilliant performance. You almost had me with your righteous indignation act."

"That was not an act, Stephan."

"It most definitely was, Roselle."

He came closer, and she took two steps back. It was unsafe to allow him too close.

"I said exactly what I was feeling," Roselle said.

Amusement filled his eyes. "Nah, you didn't. You were actually thinking about this." He wagged his tongue at her. "Or was it this?" Using both hands, he pointed at his crotch.

She refused to look and instead shot daggers at him.

"I spent the weekend thinking about you and me, and I tried to figure out if I was the only one who enjoyed our time together in and out of the bedroom so much that I couldn't stop thinking about it. I came to the conclusion that I couldn't be. You didn't fake your laughter and the happiness in your eyes when we went sight-seeing. And you sure weren't faking those moans and cries and the way you tore into my back every time I made you come. Right now you're angry because I'm calling you out, but I know you want me, which sucks because if you didn't, resisting you would be so much easier. My mother warned me away from you before we went to Paris, and I couldn't resist you. And here I am again, struggling. Happens every time I see you. I think about us making love, how responsive you are, how you give as much as you take. And it..." His voice went lower, huskier. "It's driving me out of my mind."

She also thought about their time together way more than she should. Every minute detail of the trip replayed in her head like a rewound film. She wanted to go back in time for an hour—a few minutes would suffice.

"I don't want to hear this," Roselle whispered.

"It's hard as hell, isn't it?"

She stared at the middle button on his shirt and imagined

opening each one and sliding her hands over his smooth chest and down between his legs until he moaned.

Stephan continued. "So now here we are, two people who want each other and are pretending we don't."

He advanced slowly, like a lion on the prowl, and again, she retreated. When her back hit the wall, she swallowed hard. He placed a hand above her head, and her breaths came a little faster.

Stephan leaned in closer. "What are we going to do about this thing that we started in Paris?" he asked.

"We have to be adults. We need self-control."

"When I'm near you, my control is almost non-existent. I have another idea. Why don't we keep having sex until we get tired of each other?"

"That's a terrible idea."

"One that will put us both out of our misery. Admit that staying away from each other is harder than you expected, and let's do something about it."

"Your 'something' involves having sex."

"You have a better idea? Because we're going to have sex in a few minutes, so you better speak up."

"You can't be serious. We're at work," Roselle said in a shaky voice.

"Then walk out. Otherwise, I'm going to have you up against this wall, with your legs around my waist. And you're going to have to be quiet. None of that screaming you like to do."

She wanted to leave, but the image he described made her nipples hard, and his nearness turned her knees to mush.

"Second warning, Roselle." His eyes had turned heavy-lidded with desire. "You better get out of here now, because I'm kissing you in five seconds."

"You better not," she said weakly.

Denying him was the right move to make. She should walk away. It was so easy. One foot in front of the other.

"By now, you should know I always do the opposite of what I'm told."

Neither moved, and the *pound, pound, pound* of her heart knocked against her chest in anticipation. He waited longer than five seconds, giving her plenty of time to escape. Then his face hardened with determination, and his mouth came down onto hers.

He sandwiched her between the wall and his hard body. Then his hands slid up her thighs under the pleated skirt of her dress and tilted her hips into his. An unmistakable hard-on pressed against her swollen mons with each circular grind of his hips.

She ached with need, aware of every hard muscular inch of his body, from the press of his chest to the muscled thighs beneath the well-pressed pants.

With ease, he pushed down her panties until they fell around her ankles.

"Step out," he said.

She did as he commanded, solely focused on the deep-seated need for him that wouldn't go away.

She had gone on a date with the doctor, but the entire time she compared him to Stephan. His eyes weren't whiskey-brown or filled with amusement. He made her smile but didn't make her laugh out loud the way Stephan did. And when he kissed her goodnight at the apartment door, she didn't experience a single tingle of arousal.

She sucked on Stephan's neck and listened to him groan. She thrilled at the sound that proved he was as hopelessly out of control as she was.

Stephan took out a condom and then quickly unfastened his belt and pants, letting the lot fall to the floor around his ankles. When he'd sheathed himself in protection, his hands went back under her skirt, and his fingertips grazed the lips of her sex.

Roselle gave a little cry of frustration, which prompted him to grin arrogantly.

"You're ready, aren't you?"

With his hands cradling her bare bottom, he hoisted her against the wall, and her legs went around his waist automatically as he slid between her thighs with a low grunt.

Roselle bit down on her bottom lip and closed her eyes. The only reason she didn't scream was that in the back of her mind, she remembered that they were at work and didn't want to risk being heard by an employee passing in the hall.

Stephan kicked one foot out of his pants and widened his stance. Chest heaving, he went to work, surging into her. Their breaths comingled while their bodies slid together in a sexy, decadent dance of lust. She kissed him again, demanding and eager as their tongues tangled in a heated embrace, sinking her teeth into his lush bottom lip with a feverish, darn near unquenchable desire.

Her fingers stroked over his soft hair, and she smoothed her palms down his neck and across his broad shoulders. She loved touching him and was excited by the strain of his muscles as he used his strength to hold her up as his body thrust again and again into hers.

It didn't take long for them to come. When Roselle did, her legs clamped around him, and she buried her face in his neck. She whimpered and clenched her fists behind his head to keep from screaming.

Stephan slammed a hand against the wall and held her up with one hand. He shuddered and groaned with a final thrust and then let the air out of his lungs with a mighty whoosh.

Roselle remained wrapped around him for a long spell, her head against his shoulder, his face against her neck as they struggled to slow their breathing. Finally, she released her death grip on him and lowered her feet to the floor.

Stephan dipped his head and gently kissed her mouth.

He wound her hair around his hand and tugged her flush against his body, forcing her head back, so she had to look up at him. "The rules of engagement have changed. Whenever you enter this office, close and lock the door, because any time you come in here, you're getting fucked. Whenever I come into your office, you're getting fucked. That's what we'll have to do until we can get each other out of our systems."

He sealed the deal with another kiss, harder this time, almost angrily.

Roselle whimpered as a gentle throb reemerged between her legs. At this rate, getting her fill of him could take forever.

CHAPTER 18

"*Y*ou should step back. Someone might come in here at any minute and see us," Roselle warned, placing a hand to Stephan's chest. They were alone in the break room, and though she complained, she liked being so close to him but didn't want to get caught.

"Jayson been bothering you?" Stephan asked.

"No. He's left me alone." Jayson didn't even look at her now. She felt kind of sorry for him.

"Good." His voice dropped lower. "Maybe I should close that door, and we can have a quickie."

"What! No. We can't."

"I disagree."

He reached around for the zipper on her dress.

She gasped and shoved his hand away. "Quit. What are you doing?"

"Trying to make up for lost time."

"It was five days, Stephan." She'd had to put him off when she was on her menses, and he'd acted as if the world was coming to an end.

"Felt like fifty," he said deadpan.

Roselle giggled.

He braced a hand on the counter. "I've been thinking about something. Instead of hooking up at the office or at a hotel like we did once, how about you come to my place?"

Startled, Roselle didn't know what to say at first. "Your place?" she squeaked out.

"Yeah. How about this Saturday, at seven o'clock? I'll send a car for you."

Another step closer to getting tangled in the Stephan Brooks web.

"I, um…I'll have to think about it. I usually go to see my great-aunt at the nursing home on Saturdays."

"You spend all of Saturday and Saturday night with her?"

"No," she admitted.

"Then let me ask you again, how about Saturday night at seven? I'll feed you dinner." He placed both hands on the counter, trapping her between his muscular forearms.

"Someone will see us," Roselle hissed, peeping around him.

"Better give me an answer fast, then."

"Stephan…"

"And the answer better be yes, because I'm not taking no for an answer."

"Fine! Yes!"

He grinned down at her. He was irresistible, and he made her do things that generally made her cautious. Like going to a man's house and being alone with him.

He bent to her ear. "Can't wait to taste my delicious pussy again."

Roselle closed her eyes for a split second and shuddered. No man had ever spoken to her like this. She'd never wanted them to.

Their eyes locked, and she knew he was going to kiss her, and she wanted the kiss. But then the sound of feminine laughter broke through the air, and Stephan quickly stepped back.

One of the administrative assistants from her side of the floor walked in. Phone to her ear, she cast a curious gaze at them.

Stephan cleared his throat and spoke in a loud voice. "So I'll have that file for you before the end of the day."

"Good. Thank you," Roselle said, equally loud.

Stephan walked away, but doughy knees kept her from moving. At the door, he turned to look at her one last time. With the admin's back turned to him, he licked his lips and walked out with the right corner of his mouth lifted into a sexy half-smile.

* * *

WITH AN EXTRA PEP in his step, Stephan marched into Ella's office. He'd been light-footed for a while, ever since he and Roselle had sex in his office a couple of weeks ago. They'd hooked up two more times at work and once at a nearby hotel after work, where they'd ordered room service and taken their fill of each other's bodies before going their separate ways.

Though he'd enjoyed the hours they spent together, the experiences left a bad taste in his mouth afterward. They didn't feel right.

So he'd wondered, *how would she feel about coming to my house?* That's what had prompted the invitation in the break room.

He stopped next to the settee in Ella's sitting area. She didn't notice him, preoccupied with the architectural plan she had taped to the wall.

Those must be the plans for expanding our New York office.

Stephan pulled up short. *Our* New York office, which included him. It was an odd thought, as if he were part of SJ Brands, too. He'd certainly become more entrenched in the work of the business development team, conducting his own research and running ideas by Roselle from time to time to take advantage of her knowledge base.

"You rang?" Stephan said.

Ella swung around to face him, a frown creasing her brow.

What was wrong with her?

She walked over to where he stood, chic and professional in a cream long-sleeved blouse, black wide-legged pants, and black

118

heels. Her long hair, hanging straight down her back, was secured at the nape with a diamond-studded clip.

Folding her arms, she asked, "Anything you want to tell me?"

"No. You called this meeting."

"You sure you have nothing to tell me?"

"About what?"

As far as he knew, he'd had a great couple of weeks. He'd done more research on the Brazil market by talking to a contact one of his cousins connected him to in São Paulo. It was too soon to share the results of his labor, but he was feeling really good about the progress. Not to mention, he arrived to work on time every day and hadn't fallen asleep once in any of Marcus's boring-ass meetings that would take half the time if he wasn't so wordy.

"About one of your work friends?"

Stephan's stomach tightened. *Uh-oh.* Had Jayson said something about their confrontation? Stephan knew better than to incriminate himself, so he kept this voice neutral and said, "I have no idea what you're talking about."

"Are you sleeping with Roselle?"

Stephan threw up his hands. "Whoa. How did you come to that conclusion?"

"Rumors are flying around about you two."

"In the office?"

"Where else?"

Stephan cursed softly and ran a hand over the back of his head. All he could think about was the warning Sylvie had given him before he left for France. "Has Mother heard these rumors?"

"I don't think so. Are they true?"

He waffled on whether or not to be honest, and decided not to lie. He trusted his sister. "Yes."

"Stephan!"

"I don't need a lecture." He paced away from her and rubbed his hands together. "I have to assume Mother doesn't know or she would have said something by now. I'm also pretty confident she won't find out."

"I found out, and I'm only one step below her."

Good point. A surge of panic hit him. Over a billion dollars in assets were at stake.

Had he been that sloppy? Other than yesterday, when he and Roselle were caught standing close to each other in the break room, he couldn't remember another time when they behaved in a way that justified suspicions that they were sleeping together. They didn't have lunch together anymore to ensure they didn't fuel the office rumor mill, and they were very cautious not to be seen together or addressing each other around other people. Maybe that was the problem. Had they been trying too hard? Or had Jayson complained to another employee about the warning Stephan issued to stay away from Roselle?

If Sylvie found out... Actually, he didn't want to consider the consequences if she did. His inheritance was on the chopping block.

"How did you find out?" he asked.

"I overheard a conversation in the bathroom this morning."

"Wonderful," Stephan muttered.

"The things they said about her were not nice, Stephan."

He hadn't thought about that. The stigma of sleeping together assuredly affected her more than it affected him. "What were they saying?"

"You don't want to know. And when Mother finds out, she's going to kill you."

"Okay, calm down, we're getting ahead of ourselves. You over-heard a conversation in the bathroom. Mother has her own bath-room in her office, so she won't be overhearing any gossip. And I can't see anyone going to her with relationship gossip about me. They'd be too embarrassed to tell her. I'm pretty sure I don't have anything to worry about."

That wasn't entirely true. Before the trip, a person or persons had informed her that he and Roselle had eaten lunch together. Damn snitches.

"You hope. I just have to ask you, are you insane? Mother will be furious when she finds out you slept with one of her employees. Especially Roselle."

"The chances of her finding out are low."

"But she could still find out and won't be pleased."

Stephan took a seat on one of the chairs opposite Ella's colorful settee. "You don't know the half of it. She already warned me to stay away from staff, Roselle specifically. She said she'd delay my inheritance if I didn't."

Ella's eyes widened, and her mouth fell open. "So you won't get it next year?"

Stephan shook his head.

"And you still slept with her?" Ella asked in a fierce whisper, eyes darting toward the open door.

"You wouldn't understand."

He barely understood himself. A single touch from Roselle shredded his self-control, and the soothing sound of her voice drew him in.

His legendary confidence was taking a beating. On the one hand, he liked the idea of hooking up with Roselle at his convenience, but on the other hand, he wanted to lock her down to make sure he had her to himself. Thoughts of her ran through his mind on a constant loop, and if a day went by when they didn't run into each other in the hall, he felt out of sorts.

"You're right, I don't understand such reckless behavior. Based on what you're telling me, Mother already warned you, and Roselle is one of her favorite employees. She trusts her and admires her work ethic. So good luck when she finds out."

"She's not going to find out. I got this."

"I hope you're right."

"Thanks for the vote of confidence," Stephan muttered.

"You should probably stop seeing her."

"No, thanks."

"This is serious. You should at least consider it."

"Not an option." He had no intention of stopping seeing Roselle.

"Uncle Stephan!" The excited squeals of his nieces drew his attention away from the disheartening conversation with his sister.

Ella's daughters, five-year-old Sophia and three-year-old Hannah came barreling toward him in ballet slippers and white tutus. Both girls had started taking dance classes a couple of weeks ago and immediately became obsessed with being ballerinas. They consumed everything Ella put together about famous ballerinas like Olivia Boisson, Misty Copeland, and Michaela DePrince.

Following behind them more slowly was Tyrone, Ella's husband, and the girls' stepfather. He was a light-skinned brother with a fine beard covering his jaw and chin. He and Ella met when the police department assigned him to investigate a break-in at her home.

"Hey man, what's up?" Tyrone said with a nod.

"It's all good," Stephan replied.

Tyrone must've picked up the girls from the on-site daycare downstairs. When Sylvie had expanded to take over the additional floors in the building, she added the perk of an on-site daycare for employees. Ella sometimes took advantage of the service so the girls became more socialized instead of spending all their time with their nanny. From his outside observation, they enjoyed playing and learning with other kids.

"And who do we have here? Well, if it isn't Rugrat One and Rugrat Two," Stephan said, teasing the girls with the same nickname he had given them for years.

"I'm not a Rugrat," Sophia said as she climbed up on his lap.

"Me either," Hannah said. She stood next to him on the settee and put an arm around his neck.

Stephan tugged on one of Sophia's long braids. "Are you sure about that? If you're not Rugrats, what are you then?"

"Ballerinas," Sophia answered.

Ella walked behind her desk and picked up her purse. "They love the classes, and the teacher said they're both good dancers."

"Oh boy, that means I'll have to come up with a new name for you," Stephan said.

"That's right," Sophia said, the most vocal of the two.

"Nah, I'm going to keep calling you Rugrats," Stephan said.

"No!" Hannah wailed.

"Yeah, I think that's best for now." Stephan kissed them each on their temple and set them on the floor. Standing, he asked, "Where you guys headed?"

"Late lunch around the corner," Tyrone replied. "Did you already eat? Come with us."

"No, I have work to do, and I already ate lunch."

They all started toward the door, with the girls running ahead of the three adults.

"Please consider my suggestion," Ella whispered from the side of her mouth, as they exited her office.

"Still not an option, Ella. I got this," Stephan assured her. They approached the elevator, and one of the girls had already hit the down button. The doors slid open, and they all stepped in. "I'm not worried."

"That makes one of us," Ella said.

The elevator stopped on Stephan's floor, and he walked out. "Bye, you guys have a great lunch."

"Bye!" the girls yelled at him, waving vigorously.

He waved back and let his eyes meet his sister's before he turned away and headed to his office.

CHAPTER 19

*R*oselle was actually on his doorstep in jeans and a green blouse with a big bow on the right shoulder. Her hair was styled in wavy curls that kissed her shoulders.

He braced his hands on the door frame and locked eyes with her. "You're late."

"There was an accident on the highway."

"I thought you might have canceled on me."

"Without calling? I wouldn't do that."

She clasped her hands in front of her.

"Don't tell me you're shy."

"I'm not," she said defensively, eyes widening.

"I'm not," he mimicked in a falsetto voice.

She pouted. "I shouldn't be here."

"Says who?"

"If your mother finds out, she won't be pleased. I'm an employee hooking up with her son."

She'd mentioned that concern before, which Stephan ignored.

"How will she find out if we don't tell her? Let me worry about my mother, okay? Get in here." Stephan pulled her over the threshold and into his arms.

She melted against his chest, and all was right in the world. He didn't know when it happened, but at some point, she'd become integral to his peace of mind. She was soft and smelled good, and if he didn't have dinner warming, he'd skip to the sex part of the evening.

He placed a wet kiss on her mouth, devouring her as if he hadn't seen her in months.

"Mmmm," he said when he finally released her lips.

"That's quite the greeting," she said, sounding a little breathless.

"I like my guests to feel welcomed."

"So you greet all your guests like that?"

"Only the pretty ones."

She smiled and ducked her head. He liked how she blushed so easily. It was the cutest thing.

He took her by the hand and led the way through the house. "We basically have the place to ourselves. My brother's out of town and the house manager, Paula, is upstairs in her suite. Before she went to bed, she prepared a meal of lamb chops, roasted potatoes, and spinach salad."

"Sounds great. Smells good, too. I wish I had someone to cook for me."

Roselle stopped in front of the huge half-moon shaped island. It accommodated six on the round side. The spacious kitchen was glass-enclosed and received lots of sunlight during the day. It was still light outside, so Stephan hadn't yet turned on the lights to illuminate the room.

"It's a blessing and a curse. When she treats me right, it's cool. A couple of nights ago, she made lasagna and made the noodles and sauce from scratch. Reese and I ate upstairs on the rooftop. So damn good."

"How do you stay so thin?" She propped her chin on her hand.

"Because half the time she doesn't cook for me unless I practically beg. Reese doesn't care if she cooks because he eats out most of the time. Starvation and regular exercise keep me fit."

"You have to beg your house manager to cook for you?"

"Long story short, she hates me, and I hate her." He moved around the kitchen, gathering plates and utensils.

"Why don't you hire someone else?"

Stephan laughed. "Because it's fun." He removed one of the covered dishes from the oven and placed it on the island. "You want to eat here or at the table?"

"Here is fine."

"Wine?"

"Yes, please. Let me help." Roselle hopped down off the stool, and together they moved the dishes, wine, and food to the island.

Stephan poured them each a glass of cabernet sauvignon. "Cheers," he said, holding up his glass.

She tapped hers against it. "Cheers."

He was sure he accurately read every emotion in her expressive eyes. In the past, he'd seen pain and joy. Tonight he saw contentment.

After a few minutes of eating, Roselle dabbed her mouth with a napkin. "Why is this the best lamb I've ever had?"

Stephan chuckled. "Because it probably is. She's a hell of a good cook. Actually, that's probably the real reason I can't let her go. Every time she cooks a good meal, I forget how terrible she is to me."

"You need to stay on her good side. Mmm, this meat is so tender, and it's seasoned to perfection."

"There's more if you want." Stephan pointed his fork at the top of the island where the covered dishes held extra servings.

"I couldn't." She shook her head vehemently.

"Don't act like you don't have a hearty appetite. I saw you wolf down three Nutella crepes in France."

Her eyes widened. "Really, you're going to bring that up?"

"Because you need to stop being cute and eat."

"Fine. After I'm finished, if I want more, I'll let you know."

Stephan cut into the meat. "Good. Cause I'm definitely getting seconds. And while you're asking me how I stay so fit, what about you?"

She chewed another morsel of lamb and swallowed before answering. "Genetics on both sides. My dad was tall and skinny. He passed away when I was little."

"I'm sorry. Is your mother still alive?" He'd never heard her talk about her mother, only her great-aunt, who'd taken her in when she was a teenager. He sensed something bad had happened between her and her mother, but she never divulged the details.

"Yes." Her voice held no emotion, and she gave extra attention to the spinach on her plate.

Whenever she talked about her great-aunt, she tended to get excited. Seconds ago, when she mentioned her father, her voice held sorrow. Talking about her mother injected a distinctly different tone into the conversation.

"You don't talk about her much," Stephan said carefully.

"There's not much to tell. I haven't seen her or talked to her in years." She looked up at him, almost challenging him with her eyes.

"I'm sorry. That's rough. My mother drives me nuts. She's controlling and she meddles in our lives, but I can't imagine not seeing her." He suddenly didn't feel as hungry as he did before. His heart went out to Roselle.

"Your mother gave me good advice once, and I'll never forget it. She said, 'You can't control what people say, but you can control how you react to their words. Don't ever let anyone make you feel bad about yourself.' Her words helped me through a tough period. Your mother is smart, strong, and powerful. She does whatever she wants, and no one pushes her around." She averted her eyes to the plate. "You have no idea how lucky you are."

"I love my mother, but she's no saint, you know."

"I know. But she loves you," she said in a small voice.

"She's my mother. She's supposed to."

"No." Pain flitted across her features, and he saw the same pain reflected in the brown orbs of her eyes. "Not all mothers are like that. You have a good one."

Stephan set down his fork. "Roselle, what happened?" he asked gently.

"I don't want to talk about it." She stared at her plate. She'd stopped eating, too.

"I'm not asking to be nosy. I can see that something is bothering you."

"Something is bothering me, but it's nothing I want to talk about. Not right now." Her eyes pleaded with him to understand.

Reluctantly, Stephan nodded. "Okay. Let's not talk about it."

"Thank you," she said quietly.

They finished their food, but neither ate seconds. They chose instead to indulge in a decadent dessert of warm chocolate chip brownies topped with vanilla ice cream, all piled into a large bowl. They ate every piece of brownie and emptied the plate of melted ice cream.

Afterward, Stephan dropped his spoon into the bowl. "I'm done."

"Ugh. That was so good, but it was too much." Roselle dropped her spoon in the dish, too.

"We ate a lot. We need to find a way to work off all those calories."

Their gazes locked across the countertop of the island. Stephan stood and walked over to her side.

"Let's start with a walking tour of the house. I didn't give you the grand tour," he said.

"That's right, you didn't."

"I'm a terrible host."

"Not true. You're a great host. You fed me."

He helped her down from the stool. "Let's start the tour upstairs. I'd like to show you my bedroom."

"Seems like an odd place to start a tour." She fought the amusement that pulled at the corners of her mouth.

"But I have a feeling you'll like it." He kissed her on the ear and led the way out of the kitchen.

They took the imperial staircase to the top of the landing and turned left. When they arrived at the double doors of his bedroom, he let her in first and then shut the door behind them.

He'd dimmed the lights earlier which gave the room a cozy feel. Walking up behind Roselle, he slipped his arms around her waist and whispered in her ear, "This is where the magic happens."

She giggled, leaning back into him. "That's a really large bed. I've never seen a bed that big before."

"It's a Grand King, the grand-pappy of king-size beds." It was set on a platform with two steps on each side.

"And why do you need a bed that large?"

"I..."

Not because he needed the space for himself. No, it was because a bed of that size made it more comfortable for him to sleep with multiple women at the same time.

Roselle looked over her shoulder at him. "You know what, never mind."

"Yeah, it's best not to go there." He spun her around and kissed her on the mouth. She groaned and slid her fingers under his T-shirt. Her soft hands caressed his abs and then slipped around to his back.

"Why are we doing this again? Was it to get each other out of our system?" Roselle asked.

"Exactly." He released the button on the back of her blouse and pulled the top over her head. His gaze lingered on the swell of her breasts in the black lace brassiere. "So it might take weeks. Maybe months, but I'm willing to sacrifice and put in the work, no matter how long it takes." He unsnapped the button on her jeans.

Her breath hitched. "Me too."

"Perfect. We're on the same page."

He kissed her again, with more intensity this time. One arm wound around the back of his neck while the other hand cupped the back of his head.

He was already fully hard, ready to thrust wildly into her.

"Stephan," she moaned.

That feathery plea was nearly his undoing. He practically tore off her clothes, and when they were both naked and under the sheets, he almost forgot to put on a condom. Maybe it was the excitement of having her in his house and in his bed, but he wanted her so badly his entire body felt like one painfully sensitive nerve.

When he slid home between her legs, he groaned into her neck and then his hips were in motion, driving solidly between her thighs until they were both spent and satisfied.

* * *

WHAT TIME IS IT?

Roselle looked around for a clock but saw none. It was late, no doubt. She'd probably been asleep for hours.

She stretched and then rolled onto her side to face Stephan. He lay on his side, too, facing her.

"Stephan," she whispered.

"Hmm?" he mumbled.

"I'm going to leave now."

She didn't want to. These sheets were the softest she'd ever slept on, and the mattress was extremely comfortable.

"Stay." He still hadn't opened his eyes, but he reached out and caught her wrist.

"I should go home."

His eyes fluttered open, and a frown wrinkled his brow. "You don't want to stay the night with me?"

"I do, but…" She didn't want to assume anything.

"If you stay, Paula will cook breakfast in the morning, and I won't starve."

"I feel like you're in an abusive relationship with this woman."

He laughed softly. "I am, but you can save me, and I'll have food to eat tomorrow. She'll cook if a guest is here."

She didn't know if he was kidding or serious.

"Stay and let me give you a couple more orgasms and put your ass to sleep," he said in a low voice.

She couldn't argue with that logic. She climbed on top of him, and he grew hard against her inner thigh.

"Can I ride this time?"

His eyes darkened with lust. "You can ride any time you want, sweetness."

Their lips locked together and his hands smoothed down her back to cup her backside. Grinding against him, she kissed him greedily. When the time came, and she sank down on top of his hard dick, her head fell back as indescribable pleasure vibrated up her spine.

Possessing him, owning him, she moved up and down and demanded her pleasure. And he gave so much that when the orgasm ricocheted throughout her insides, she cried out in a loud voice and collapsed on top of him, breathing heavy through her nose and mouth.

The last thing she remembered before she fell asleep was Stephan pulling her close and covering her with the sheet.

CHAPTER 20

"Hi, Auntie!" Roselle leaned down and kissed her great-aunt's leathery cheek.

Betty coughed into the handkerchief in her hand. She'd caught a summer cold that she struggled to shake. Each time she thought it was gone, it returned a week later.

"You're mighty chipper today," Betty said, eyeing Roselle.

"I'm always chipper."

"Not like this. You have a lot more pep in your step lately. You're different."

A few of the employees at work had made similar comments. She felt different, but what did they see?

"How am I different?" Roselle asked, sitting in the chair beside her aunt.

Her aunt pursed her lips as she thought. "You laugh more. In general, your spirits seem up. I can't put my finger on exactly when I noticed the change. Wait, I know! I noticed the change in you not too long after you returned from Paris."

"Then I guess you can say Paris changed me."

Not just Paris. Her transformation started there and continued stateside after she and Stephan continued to see each other, make love, talk, share, and laugh.

Right now, he was in New York with Marcus, checking out the SJ Brands showrooms, meeting with staff, and learning more about retail merchandising. She missed him so much. He might have an ego the size of Jupiter, but he treated her with such care, making her feel special and wanted in a way she hadn't before. Or at least she'd never allowed herself to feel because she'd been too busy protecting herself from opening up to anyone so she'd avoid pain. She didn't have to worry about that with him.

Stephan pushed and pushed hard, past her boundaries and into the cracks and crevices of her heart. He made her uncomfortable while putting her at ease, and for the first time in a long time, she felt alive. Really alive, like she wasn't merely going through the motions. She wanted more of that, more of him.

"Paris, huh?" her aunt asked with a heavy dose of skepticism on her face.

"Yes, Paris." Roselle handed Betty her latest gift. The small box contained a pair of gloves that had been discontinued because they didn't sell well, but they were a lovely shade of pink, a color her aunt adored.

"Don't try to distract me with your gift. I'll get to that later. I want to know what has you giggling and smiling all the time. What in the world happened in Paris?"

Roselle folded her arms. "Why are you all up in my business, auntie?"

"Because I know you have something juicy to tell me, and you better go on ahead and tell me before I pop you upside the head."

Roselle heaved an exaggerated heavy sigh. "Okay, I'll tell you about Paris. Promise not to judge."

"Honey, when have I ever judged you?"

While the remark sounded like a throwaway comment, her ability to reserve judgment had been what saved Roselle's mental health years ago. Her support and acts of kindness ensured Roselle did not feel alone in the world during the toughest period of her life.

"Never," Roselle answered.

She launched into the story about what happened between her and Stephan in Paris, fading to black on the parts where she spent the nights in his arms. She also told her aunt about their current relationship and how much she enjoyed spending time with him.

"Well, this Stephan sounds like quite a character."

Roselle laughed. "He is, but he's not as bad as he comes across. I'm not sure he realizes what a kind soul he is."

"You're in love with him, aren't you?"

"In love?" Roselle shook her head vigorously. "No way. I'm having fun and enjoying myself."

"I know what love looks like, baby. The question is, how serious is this relationship? If it ended tomorrow, will you be okay?"

She didn't want to think about their relationship ending and honestly hadn't thought that far ahead. The very thought pained her so much that her mind constantly skittered away from the possibility of losing Stephan. If that happened, running into him at work would be unbearable.

"I'm sure I'll be okay," she said to her aunt. She forced a bright smile, but her aunt had always told her she saw through all of her false emotions. Her eyes were too expressive. They truly were the window to her soul.

"I'm not saying you can't enjoy yourself, because you definitely deserve it. You work hard, you take care of me and make sure that I have everything I need—"

"I'm happy to do it. You took care of me, and we're family. We have each other."

Betty coughed into the handkerchief again. "We do have each other, and that will never change. I know that you're happy to take care of me, but what I'm saying is, are you emotionally prepared to have the kind of relationship you deserve? Will you tell him everything?"

She'd already thought about it and wanted to tell Stephan about the rape and what she went through as a result—being ostracized by friends and people she cared about. Her own mother had turned her back.

But did she and Stephan really have that kind of relationship? Sharing something so personal was not easy. It took her years to work up the courage to talk to a therapist about her ordeal, instead crawling into herself and staying away from other people.

Therapy helped her understand her misplaced guilt, and how it kept her in a protective shell—to never make a mistake, so there would be no consequences afterward. If she told Stephan, he might feel the same as other people did. He might blame her, too. He might say she used poor judgment that night, and if he looked at her in that way, she couldn't take it.

"You don't have to rush," Betty said gently.

"I know. But the truth is, I'm not sure we'll last, and I don't want to drop that bomb into our relationship."

Three years ago, she opened up to her boyfriend at the time because she'd been called to testify in a case where Charles's widow was the defendant. While her boyfriend didn't come right out and blame her, he asked the usual questions.

You barely knew him, so why did you leave with him?

What did you think was going to happen?

Their relationship became strained. Then she took the stand at the trial. More guilt closed in. Tight. Suffocating. Could she have done something to prevent those other women from being hurt? How many others were there? After a time, she stopped eating.

Sylvie Johnson didn't know it, but she helped her through that tough period. Her aunt gave her love and compassion, but Sylvie showed her how to be strong.

"You can't control what people say, but you can control how you react to their words. Don't ever let anyone make you feel bad about yourself."

She went back into therapy, changed her clothes, changed her hair, started eating again. It took time, but she gradually returned to her former self.

"Do you trust him?" her aunt asked.

Did she? If she had to ask, maybe she didn't.

135

"I'm not sure." The truth was, she didn't trust anyone completely, except her aunt.

"I don't want to see you get hurt, so if you're not sure, then you should definitely wait."

Her throat tightened, and she sat back in the chair.

"I didn't mean to bring you down, baby."

"You didn't."

"I want you to be safe. I want you to stop hiding and have the happiness you deserve. It's long overdue."

"I am happy. Stephan makes me happy."

"Good."

"He, um, he invited me to the opening of a lounge in Charlotte. His cousin Trenton and his wife Alannah are going to be there. Trenton invested in the club and opened it with one of their fraternity brothers. Stephan's flying up there in a couple of weeks and wants me to go with him. I want to, but...I don't know."

"You should go, baby."

"We'll be gone all weekend."

"And?" Betty tutted. "You better not turn him down because you have to come see me. Isn't that why I'm in this nursing home? So someone can always keep an eye on me when you're not around?" She coughed into the handkerchief. "Take a weekend off from sitting with your old wrinkly aunt. If that man is inviting you to meet his family, he must be serious about you."

"I don't know if he is, but I'm nervous."

"Nothing to be nervous about. And by the way, when you get back, I want to meet Mr. Stephan, who has my niece grinning from ear to ear so often."

"You're not going to give him a hard time, are you?" Roselle asked teasingly. She took her aunt's hand in hers.

"Maybe a little bit."

They both laughed.

"I want you to meet him, too," Roselle said quietly.

Betty squeezed her hand. "Go to Charlotte and have fun. Do all the things I wish I had done when I was your age. Have fun for the both of us. Deal?"

"Deal."

Roselle was excited about the trip, but her aunt had given her food for thought. Her feelings for Stephan ran very deep. She could very well be in love with him already, as her aunt suggested.

But how did he feel about her?

CHAPTER 21

*R*oselle wished her belly would cooperate.

She walked beside Stephan from the car to the building entrance, tugging on her dress and wondering if she should have worn something else. No matter how down to earth Stephan said his cousin and wife were, she wanted to make a good impression. Yet there was absolutely no reason why she should be *this* nervous about meeting Stephan's family. Except doing so was a big step, particularly since they'd never been out in public as a couple. He was worried about his mother finding out about them, and so was she. She didn't think Sylvie would appreciate one of her employees having an affair with her son.

Usually, Roselle went over to Stephan's place, and they ate dinner together or watched a movie in his theater room. Somehow he managed to get advanced screenings of a couple of films weeks before they hit the theaters. If they stayed up late playing video games—during which he mercilessly kicked her ass—he'd call the concierge service and have them arrange delivery of a late-night snack and drinks and then they'd be good to go for another couple of hours.

A few times they hung out with his brother Reese and his latest female friend at the indoor pool or ate dinner at the island in the kitchen. Roselle had become good friends with Paula, the house manager, and thought the love-hate relationship between her and Stephan was hilarious, though at times he did not.

They entered the lounge, christened The Underground Charlotte because Seattle already had a The Underground, and Roselle's mouth fell open. Stephan had shown her the before photos. They'd done a fantastic job renovating the old warehouse because the building looked nothing like a warehouse now. It didn't have the same atmosphere as the club they went to in France. On the contrary, there was a more relaxed vibe, with the DJ playing old-school R&B and the small, assembled crowd mostly bobbing their heads.

Purple and blue lights made the dark interior glow, assisted by a line of outrageously large chandeliers that ran the length of the building. One half of one wall was a long bar with backless stools lit up from the floor with iridescent blue lights. There was a dance floor, plenty of tables, and lounging areas filled with circular sofas and soft-cushioned chairs.

Overall, the trendy, contemporary design was the perfect meeting place for an after-work crowd or the weekend crowd looking for low-key fun to get into.

Since the place wasn't packed yet, they quickly found Stephan's cousin, Trenton, and his wife, Alannah. They sat on one of the circular sofas, facing the dance floor. Trenton rested his arm on the back of the chair and was leaning in, talking to his wife. Roselle didn't have a good view of him from her vantage point as they approached, but the minute Stephan came into Trenton's line of sight, he jumped up from the sofa.

"Look who dragged himself from Atlanta!" He pulled Stephan into a hug.

Stephan chuckled. "Yeah, right. I leave Atlanta all the time. When was the last time you left Seattle?"

"I leave all. The. Time. This must be Roselle. Nice to meet you."

Wow. She was blown away by Trenton's looks. If she weren't already halfway in love with Stephan, she could have easily fallen under his cousin's spell. He was seriously good-looking, had the same roguish smile as Stephan and what seemed to be green eyes, but it was hard to tell in the darkness of the club.

"Nice to meet you." She shook his hand.

"And who is this beautiful lady?" Stephan asked.

He pulled Alannah to her feet and into his embrace. Alannah was light-skinned, with her long, auburn hair secured on top of her head in a loose top knot.

Stephan stepped back and surveyed his cousin's wife with a grin on his face. "Look at you," he said.

She placed a hand on her expanded waistline. "Yes, look at me. I'm huge. Five months pregnant and everyone thinks I'm at least seven." She sighed.

"What are you having again?"

"We decided we didn't want to know the gender of the baby," she replied.

"By we, she means she," Trenton said.

"I like the idea of being surprised," she conceded.

"Are you doing one of those gender-reveal parties?" Roselle asked.

"Absolutely not. I had to put my foot down somewhere," Trenton said.

Alanna rolled her eyes. "I'm still working on him." She directed a sweet smile at her husband.

Right as Trenton opened his mouth to respond, one of their frat brothers let out a Kappa Alpha Sigma call. No less than twelve men responded, including Stephan and Trenton. The dance floor then became the center of attention as men poured from various corners of the club.

"Ladies, if you will excuse us," Trenton said.

"Keep an eye on my baby," Stephan said to Alannah, before hurrying off.

Both women sat down on the sofa and watched the men do the Kappa Alpha Sigma stroll on the dance floor—a series of moves that included shoulder shimmies, gyrating hips, and letting their tongues hang out suggestively.

"So how did you meet Stephan?" Alannah asked.

Now that they were seated together, Roselle noticed the freckles sprinkled on her nose.

"We work together."

"Oh." Alannah frowned. "Stephan works?"

"Yes. He works at SJ Brands headquarters in the business development department."

"I had no idea. I'm sure Trenton knows, but he didn't mention it."

"How did you and Trenton meet?"

Alannah rubbed her belly, a soft smile on her lips. "Long story. We've known each other since we were kids and were friends for years. Eventually, we moved past being friends."

"So you've known Stephan for a long time, too?"

"Oh yeah. I was practically part of the family, so I went on trips with them and I know Ella and Simone and Reese—everyone, really well."

Roselle fell silent. The Kappa Alpha Sigmas were now chanting and throwing up hand signs, their loud voices overshadowing the music.

"Something you want to ask me?" Alannah asked.

There was, but she didn't know Alannah at all and didn't know if the question was appropriate.

"You can ask. I promise it'll stay between us."

After a brief hesitation, Roselle asked, "Okay, what were Stephan's other girlfriends like?"

"Honestly... I don't know that he's had other girlfriends. Not serious ones, anyway. I've met other women at a party here and there, but... I wouldn't call them girlfriends, and they'd never come to anything like this. He likes to go to places where he can show off and show them off."

"Oh." Roselle's shoulders slumped.

"No, no, no. You're taking what I said the wrong way."

Alannah placed a reassuring hand on Roselle's wrist. "I mean that this event might be too low-key for the women he typically hangs around, and maybe I'm wrong, but you seem kind of quiet."

"I am," Roselle admitted.

"That's what I thought. So he's probably likely to stay here longer with you, but if you were a different type of person, he'd swing through, show his face to be supportive—maybe post a few pics on Instagram—and then leave again." Alannah leaned in. "Can I tell you something else?"

"Sure."

"I've never heard him call any other woman 'my baby.'"

"Never?" Roselle asked, a quick thrill running through her.

"Never," Alannah assured her. Then she slid back into her own space.

Too bad Alannah didn't live in Atlanta. Roselle had a feeling they'd get along well.

* * *

"DON'T THINK I didn't see the way you looked at my cousin," Stephan said from the bathroom, where he had the door open and was brushing his teeth. He had rented a suite at one of the luxury hotels in downtown Charlotte.

"What?" Roselle looked up from the iPad in her hand, where she lay under the covers.

After Stephan and his frat brothers kicked off the party, other people went out onto the dance floor. A little after midnight, the place became packed, the music was hot, and the drinks were flowing. Stephan deejayed for a bit, and then Roselle joined him and the other lounge-goers on the dance floor.

The relaxed atmosphere made it easy to mingle and talk, and their corner was a hotspot where folks came and chilled for a while, had a few drinks and good conversation, and then moved on. They left after two in the morning and joined Alannah and Trenton for pancakes and waffles at a local eatery before going their separate ways.

The plan was to spend Saturday and Sunday morning sightseeing before flying back to Atlanta Sunday afternoon.

"You have a type," Stephan said, speaking over brushing his teeth.

"I do not."

"Your favorite rappers are T.I. and LL Cool J. You like Michael Ealy and also *love*—your word—Kendrick Sampson. Tonight you were drooling over my cousin. Coincidence? I think not. I rest my case."

She giggled. "That doesn't mean I have a type."

"Uh-huh." He turned off the light and came into the room, completely naked and thoroughly confident. He always slept naked and wanted her to do the same. Sometimes she indulged him when it was right after they made love, but otherwise, she wore a nightshirt or one of his many T-shirts to sleep in. Tonight she was going to sleep in her underwear, and one of his old T-shirts emblazoned with the words: *If I said you have a beautiful body, would you hold it against me?*

He slid under the covers and lay back against her chest. Though he was reclining against her, he didn't feel heavy. His body was a comforting weight.

Stephan took the tablet and scrolled through the report she'd brought up on the screen.

Roselle pointed at the figures in one of the tables. "As you can see, there was a sharp decline in the Brazilian market that year. Fifteen percent is a lot." He'd said her insights were invaluable, so she shared her opinions often.

"Yeah," Stephan said slowly. "And that was after the launch of the new line?"

"Yes. We were never able to penetrate that market for some reason."

He continued scrolling until he came to the end of the report. He swiped to the next one.

"If you don't have a type, what do you like about me?"

Stephan asked, picking up their conversation from earlier.

"You make me laugh."

She slid a hand repeatedly over his head, gently rubbing his soft hair. He liked it when she did that, and she could already feel him relaxing further as excess tension oozed from his body.

"So I'm a joke to you?" Stephan asked.

"No." Roselle lightly pinched the muscle in his shoulder. "What do you like about me?"

He was quiet for a while, and the wait for an answer seemed to take an hour instead of only seconds. Finally, he set down the iPad and twisted onto his side, resting on his elbow and looking directly into her eyes.

"Your smart, sweet, and sexy." All playfulness was gone from his face. "I think more when I'm with you. The truth is, I haven't always made the right decisions. You make me want to do right."

Such an honest answer deserved an honest answer in return. Roselle trailed a finger down the middle of his chest. "I love your body, you really do make me laugh, and you're considerate. I don't feel alone or afraid when I'm with you, and you make me...you make me want to stop hiding."

She kissed him softly on the mouth, and he cupped her jaw, deepening the kiss. She breathed into his mouth as desire crawled through her veins. Stephan helped her out of the T-shirt and tossed it to the floor. Then his thumbs hooked in the waistband of her panties, and she helped him push them down her legs.

"I keep telling you to stop wearing panties to bed. Four out of five gynecologists say you should let the vagina breathe at night." His breath was fresh and smelled like wintergreen toothpaste.

Roselle smiled against his lips and kissed his mouth some more. "I'm pretty sure that's not a thing."

He sucked the sensitive part of her neck, and she gasped as shivers spattered over her skin. "I'm pretty sure it is. I keep telling you that, but you don't believe me."

"Because you made it up. You're not a doctor."

He lifted his head and frowned at her indignantly. "I don't brag about my medical degree, but my specialty is gynecology, and my colleagues and I have determined the vagina needs air at night—especially when you're lying in bed with me." He flashed a sexy grin. "You may call me Dr. Brooks. I'm here to help."

He kissed a path down her stomach to between her legs, stroking his tongue through the wet folds and kissing her lower lips with the same affection he did her upper ones. Roselle writhed under the ministrations of his mouth until he kissed his way back up her stomach, sucking on her nipples and teasing them with his tongue.

"I swear that pussy tastes better every time. You got me addicted, girl," he whispered.

His mouth covered hers, but Roselle pushed him onto his back and took control of the kiss, while Stephan's fingers started playing with her clit. She ground her hips into his hand, so horny and anxious for the joining of their bodies.

Her aunt was right. She was falling in love with him. The intoxicating newness of love formed a heady rush of heat and excitement. It had to be the best, scariest feeling in the whole world.

The tip of his shaft nudged the cleft between her legs. The next time he teasingly prodded her entrance, a fit of recklessness spurred her into action, and she sank onto him, eyes rolling back at the splendor of his raw possession.

Stephan gasped and froze, his fingers sinking into her ass. "*Fuck.*"

He flipped her onto her back and pounded into her as if he'd been waiting for this very opportunity to claim her. He knew better, she knew better, but in the heat of the moment, none of that mattered. Not when her desire for him beat like a bass drum in her loins.

Hooking his arms behind her knees, he pressed them back to her chest. She clung to him, clasping the back of his head, arching into each powerful thrust. Head thrown back, she drowned in a sea of emotion, savoring all the textures of his skin—the hardness of his chest, the tickle of his hair-rough thighs, the strength in his arms as he pinned her to the bed.

As the orgasm slowly built, her cries of pleasure matched his animalistic growls. She splintered soon after, her feminine muscles quivering around him. Then Stephan came too, grinding his hips into hers, burying himself deep and hard. He swore again, shuddered, and then let out a deep-chested groan before dropping his head to her shoulder.

Exhausted but satisfied, she turned her head and kissed his temple.

CHAPTER 22

*R*oselle awoke with a start. She blinked, eyes adjusting to the dark before she remembered where she was. At a hotel in Charlotte, with Stephan. As she became aware of her surroundings, she also became aware of Stephan's deep breathing and his arm thrown across the back of her waist.

Her heart was racing.

What had woken her up? A dream? She couldn't remember, but a heavy, oppressive energy in the air warned that something was wrong. But what?

She swallowed and took a few deep breaths to calm the energetic pounding of her heart. As the frantic beating settled, a need to call her Aunt Betty came out of nowhere and formed a knot as big and tight as a closed fist.

They'd talked before she left on her trip. Her summer cold had returned and morphed into bronchitis, and the infection turned into pneumonia. Roselle had been ready to cancel her plans, but at her great-aunt's insistence, came on the trip with Stephan. She talked to her once when they landed and again before they went to The Underground Charlotte. She had sounded much better, and the on-staff nurse confirmed to Roselle that she was definitely on the mend.

The weird feeling she had was probably nothing, but she needed to put her mind at ease. Slowly, she slid from under Stephan's arm and eased off the mattress so as not to wake him. She slipped back on his T-shirt and picked up her phone from the table in the corner where it was charging.

She quietly closed the door to the bedroom and sat in one of the armchairs. She dialed the number for Covent Gardens and waited for someone to answer.

"Hello?" The voice was vaguely familiar.

"Hello, this is Roselle Parker. This is going to sound weird, but I called to check on my great-aunt and make sure that she's okay. Her name is Betty Parker."

"Oh, hi, Roselle. This is Stacy. I checked on your aunt a couple of hours ago, and she was doing fine. Do you still want me to check on her?"

"Yes, if you don't mind. It will make me feel better."

"Sure thing, honey. I'll go upstairs now and call you back in a few minutes, okay? What's your number?"

Roselle gave it to her and said, "Thanks. I appreciate this so much."

Clutching the phone to her chest, Roselle closed her eyes and rested the back of her head against the chair. If her aunt had been fine two hours ago, then she was probably fine now. She laughed to herself at her silly overreaction. She'd probably come awake because of a dream she immediately forgot upon waking up. Probably one of those dreams where she was falling off a cliff or something.

She continued to wait, bouncing one leg over the other.

What was taking so long? Had Stacy misplaced her number that fast?

One at a time, she rubbed her clammy hands on the chair fabric and stared at the phone's dark screen, frowning. "A few more minutes." Then she'd call back.

Two minutes later, the phone rang, and she immediately answered. "Hello?"

"Hello, Roselle?" Stacy didn't sound the way she had sounded when she hung up before. Her voice sounded strained, and Roselle was immediately on alert. She sat up straight and held the phone tightly to her ear.

"Yes?"

"Honey, I'm so sorry…" Her voice broke.

Her stomach twisted in protest. "No, go back. Did you go to the right room? Betty Parker. B-E-T-T-Y—"

"Roselle, I'm sorry, but she's—"

"No!" Roselle screamed. She didn't want to hear it. Despite sensing something was wrong, she couldn't bear to hear the words. "No!"

* * *

STEPHAN SAT UP, blinking the sleep from his eyes.

"No!"

That was Roselle's voice, sounding cracked and broken.

He hopped up naked from the bed and ran to the door. He yanked it open and laid eyes on Roselle, who had collapsed onto the floor on her haunches, bent over as if in physical pain.

He dropped to his knees before her and placed a comforting hand on her back. "Roselle, what's wrong?"

She looked up at him, tears streaming down her face. "It's—it's my Aunt Betty." She held a death grip on the phone.

"Hello? Hello, Roselle?" a female voice on the other line said.

"Give me the phone, babe," Stephan said gently.

She stared at him with unseeing eyes. She seemed to have gone into shock, so he took one end of the phone and gently tugged. She released it but remained numb, staring at the window across the room, emptiness in her eyes.

"Hello," he said.

"Hello, this is Stacy at Covent Gardens nursing home. Is Roselle…is she okay?"

He glanced at her. She appeared to be in a catatonic state, frozen.

"No, she's not," he said.

"I'm so sorry. To get this news in the middle of the night is devastating, and I know the type of relationship Roselle and her Aunt Betty had. We dialed 911, but it's obvious it's already too late. At some point during the night, Miss Betty took a turn for the worst. She's gone."

Oh no.

He had never met Roselle's aunt, but she talked about her a lot, and it was clear that she considered to be her mother. He could only imagine her devastation.

"Tell her I'm sorry. We're all sorry. We loved Miss Betty." He heard tears in the woman's voice.

"I'll let her know."

Stephan hung up the phone. "Babe, look at me." He took Roselle's chin in his hand.

She blinked and focused on him.

Stephan took both of her hands in his. "We need to fly back to Atlanta right away. Let's get our stuff together and I'll see about getting a flight down there immediately, okay?"

She nodded.

That was better than before. At least the catatonic freeze was no longer in place.

Stephan helped her to her feet, but her hands tightened on his. "They made a mistake, right? Stacy… She doesn't know what she's talking about. My aunt is fine. She was fine before we left Atlanta, and she was fine when they checked on her two hours ago."

"Babe—"

"We can go to Atlanta right away, but I'm going to be very upset with them for causing me so much stress when there's nothing wrong with my aunt."

Stephan cupped her face in his hands. "Babe, you heard what she said, right? She's gone."

Her lower lip trembled and fresh tears shimmered in her eyes.

"They're not wrong. This is real," Stephan said softly. If he could, he'd take away her pain, stuff it inside his own body to make her feel better.

Her face crumpled. "Not her. She's all I have in the world. She's all I have, Stephan."

Stephan shook his head. "No, she's not. You've got me, too." He pulled her into his arms, and she sobbed against his bare chest.

"I'm here, babe. I got you, okay? I got you."

CHAPTER 23

$\mathcal{T}$he knocking started again, and Roselle had a feeling she knew who stood on the opposite side of the door. Stephan.

She hadn't seen him since the funeral on Saturday. She could leave him out there, ignore the knocking the way she'd ignored his calls over the past three days that she'd missed work. But the truth was, they needed to talk.

Her therapist would say she was punishing herself. Cutting herself off from the man she loved over the guilt of leaving her aunt alone when she was sick, and having her die without Roselle by her side.

"It's okay to be happy. You don't have to punish yourself," he'd say.

Then he'd tell her to journal or meditate. But she hadn't journaled in years, and she didn't want to meditate. She wanted to face the death of her aunt head-on.

Dragging herself from bed, Roselle quickly splashed water on her face, went to the door, and opened it. As she suspected, Stephan stood outside. He was in the process of dialing, probably her number because she hadn't answered the door quickly enough. She wouldn't have received the call, though. She'd turned off her phone and buried it in the bottom of a drawer.

"Hi," she said.

"Hey." Concern filled his eyes. "Babe, what's going on? I've been trying to reach you for the past three days. I was worried. Why haven't you returned my calls?"

"I've been busy."

"Can I help?"

Roselle shook her head. "No."

"Can I do anything? Is there anything you need?"

She didn't respond. Having him here made her happy and sad at the same time. Happy, because she loved his company—because she loved *him*. But sad, because she knew what she had to do and didn't want to. The thought of breaking up made her weepy.

"Let me in, and we can talk," Stephan said gently.

Roselle stepped aside. He came in, and she rested her back against the closed door. Concern remained in Stephan's eyes, and she straightened her shoulders. "You won't like what I'm about to say."

He swallowed as if he already anticipated the words. "Before you make any drastic decisions—"

"I want to be alone, Stephan."

"Babe, listen to me." He reached for her, but she pulled back, and his hand fell away.

"You didn't do anything wrong, but I've been thinking since the funeral, about our relationship."

He remained silent, his body tensing almost imperceptibly.

"It takes up a lot of my time."

"We can dial things back. We see each other at work every day, then several times a week you're at my house. Sometimes you spend the whole weekend. It's a lot. I get it. We don't have to see each other as often."

He was being so accommodating, which made what she had to do so hard.

"I didn't have to take that trip to Charlotte with you. If I hadn't,

I would have been here when my great-aunt passed and she wouldn't have been alone during her final hours." The guilt tore her up inside. Ruthless, unyielding, punishing in its brutality.

"You shouldn't blame yourself in any way for not being here when she passed. What happened to her was a tragedy. There's no reason—"

"I need a break from you, from us, from this relationship. It's too much."

His eyes turned bleak. "For how long?"

Her heart cracked into a thousand pieces. "Indefinitely," she said quietly. It pained her to say that word. It was so final.

"That's not a break. You're ending our relationship. Talk to me, Roselle. Did I screw something up?"

She shook her head. "It's not you, it's me."

"Then let me help you."

"*Stop*. I don't want your help. I can handle this on my own. Please, stop."

"You want me to walk away and pretend like our relationship means nothing? It's over, just like that?"

"Why are you doing this?"

"I care about you."

"We're different. We come from different worlds and have different needs. You have all these friends and acquaintances and family. My aunt is gone, and she's all I had."

"You keep saying that, and I'm standing right here!" He slammed a fist against his chest.

"The person I loved most in the world died. This is real life, Stephan. Not another party or club opening."

His eyebrows arrowed down in anger. "What does that mean? You think that's all I'm about?"

"What do you have to worry about except looking good and having a good time? Your job at SJ Brands isn't even real. If you walk away from the business development department at any time, you'll still be fine. You're rich and live a privileged life."

Color tinged the top of his cheekbones, and he let out a bitter laugh. "That's what you think of me? I'm a pretty boy whose life is easy? I don't have to work, and I sure as heck don't understand pain, right? You really think I'm that shallow?"

"I'm not saying you're shallow. I'm saying, what have you had to suffer through? Have you ever had to struggle?"

Stephan fell quiet, which was very unlike him. He stared at his shoes, and an uncomfortable, awkward silence engulfed them. When he finally looked at her, he'd turned off all emotion. Was he angry, disappointed, had she hurt him?

"In case you don't know, different people deal with pain and loss in different ways. Yes, I have life easier than most, and I don't deny that. But I watched my parents hurt each other for a long time before they divorced. Then I watched my mother struggle to be whole again after the man she loved left. *I* struggled because I didn't have my father around anymore. My Uncle Cyrus died in the hospital after a drunk driver hit his limo. My Uncle Anthony was murdered by his wife. And that's just on my mother's side of the family."

"Stephan, I'm sorry. I—"

"No, let me finish. So maybe I don't act like I know pain, but I do know pain. And for you, of all people to say those things to me, when you know me. I let you inside my life, inside my world, in a way I've never let another woman. I've opened up to you—" He stopped abruptly and took a deep breath, biting down on his bottom lip. "I wanted to be here for you, that's all. That's why I came. But you don't need me. You don't need anybody."

"I'm sorry for what I said, but going our separate ways is for the best."

He walked up and stood in front of her. "Got it. Step aside so I can leave."

She stared up into whiskey-colored eyes devoid of emotion. "Stephan—"

"No need to say another word. We're different. Step aside." He averted his eyes from hers and stared at the wall beside the door as if he no longer wanted to look at her.

Roselle moved out of the way, and Stephan opened the door and walked out. She stood in the entry for a few minutes, numb.

Then, with a small cry, she rushed into her bedroom and fell onto the bed. She hugged her pillow, burying her face in its softness. Quiet sobs rocked her body.

Her Aunt Betty was gone for good. Stephan was gone.

She was really all alone now.

* * *

SEATED AT HIS DESK, Stephan stared at his watch. He really wanted to skip this meeting with his mother, but when Sylvie Johnson called, you answered, and you showed up on time.

He shoved out of the chair and exited the office. In the main hallway, he avoided looking on the creatives side where Roselle worked. She was back in the office after being out for a week. He knew because, of course, he saw her this morning as they were both walking into the building. They took the elevator up with the rest of the employees and exited on their floor without a single word to each other. Like strangers. Like they hadn't lain in his bed together, laughing and talking and making passionate love.

The memories refused to leave him. They remained in the background, constant, like white noise. Torturing him day and night.

The universe had done a great job of kicking his butt lately. Maybe this was its way of balancing things out after all the dirt he'd done and gotten away with.

The elevator opened, and Jayson came out wearing a suit and carrying a briefcase. He pulled up short. "Excuse me," he said, sidestepping Stephan.

"Hey, Jayson."

He turned around.

"Listen, I... I owe you an apology for what happened in the break room a while back. I should have never come at you like that about Roselle. I apologize for my behavior."

A few seconds ticked by as Jayson stared at him in surprise. "Oh. That's okay, man."

"Nah, it's not okay, and I know that. Do you accept my apology?"

"Sure. Thanks." His face contained a mixture of surprise and confusion.

"Cool." Since the elevator doors had closed, Stephan hit the button again. It was still on their floor, so they popped open, and he stepped into the cabin.

"Hey, Stephan. You, um… you want to go to lunch sometime?"

What was it about this dude and lunch?

Stephan held the doors open and was about to decline, but Jayson looked so anxious, he didn't have the heart to turn him down. "Yeah, let's do lunch some time."

His face broke out into a wide grin. "Cool, man. All right, then."

"But Jayson, do me a favor. None of your crass jokes, okay?"

"Oh no, man, I hear you. I'm done with all of that. I don't do that anymore."

Stephan doubted that, but he nodded. "Good to know. I'll holler at you, and we'll hook up, maybe later this week."

"Yeah, yeah. Let me know when."

Stephan stepped back and let the doors close. "I hope I don't regret that," he said to himself.

On the top floor, he walked into the reception area of his mother's office.

"Hi, Inez."

"Hi, Stephan. Go right in. She's expecting you."

"Thanks."

Stephan knocked once and entered his mother's office. She stood with her butt resting against the edge of her glass desk, arms folded, apparently waiting for him.

He walked slowly toward her. "You wanted to see me?"

Hands on her hips, Sylvie took several steps and came to stand directly in front of him. She glared at him through her glasses. "Are you sleeping with Roselle?"

The blunt question caught him off guard. "What? I—"

"You're sleeping with her. That's all I needed to know. Thank you." She stalked to the other side of her desk.

"I'm not." Not anymore.

"You're lying. Did you really think I wouldn't hear the rumors about you and her? Apparently, this has been going on for quite some time, right under my nose. We're done here. Goodbye. Go back to work. I only needed confirmation that you'd broken our agreement."

"Mother, it wasn't much of an agreement. You made the rules, and I had to go along with them."

"That's the way life works. The person with the money makes the rules, which you have broken, I might add." She picked up the phone.

"What are you doing?"

"Calling my attorney."

"Wait!" Stephan yanked away the phone and slammed it back in the cradle. They stared at each other across the desk. "I screwed up, but she and I aren't together anymore. She broke up with me."

"Or you would still be sleeping with her?" Sylvie arched a brow.

Stephan nodded. "Yes," he admitted reluctantly. No point in lying.

Sleeping with her. Laughing with her. Eating with her. Doing whatever she wanted because it was enough to spend time with her. He wanted to do everything with her and for her. He used to hate when people asked him for money or favors but learned he hated not being asked even more. He wanted to spoil Roselle and take care of her, but she wouldn't let him.

"But we're done, for good. I haven't slept with anyone else in the company. I swear. Would you reconsider?"

"Why should I?"

"Because I've changed. I know you don't believe me, but I

have. Not only that, I actually like working here. It's challenging, but I'm learning a lot. I want to stay in business development."

"Marcus told me you're working on expansion ideas for Brazil?"

"Yes. It's a work in progress, but I'm almost finished."

Sylvie sat down and studied him in silence. Stephan didn't move, holding her gaze and silently praying for forgiveness.

"I'll think about it," she finally said. She lifted her iPad from the desk and swiveled in her chair so that she faced the window, away from Stephan.

That was her way of dismissing him, and he knew better than to argue or continue talking. He'd leave her alone. At least he'd managed to stop her from calling the attorney—for now.

He left the office in a worse mood than he arrived.

At this point, he wanted to go to sleep and never wake up.

CHAPTER 24

*S*tephan's arm and leg muscles burned, but every time he thought about quitting, he did another lap. His head twisted to the side every so often to catch a breath as he sliced through the water in the Olympic-sized pool.

When he reached the far end, he doubled back again.

One more lap, he thought. Pushing his body to the limit meant less time thinking about Roselle.

He sluiced through the water with easygoing strokes, moving slower now that the strain of fatigue had entered his limbs. When he arrived at the other end, he looked up and saw his brother Reese and his cousin Malik, standing on the pavement. Malik was the son of their father's half-brother. Big, bearded, and with copper skin, he worked as a metal sculptor and was currently in a relationship with one of Stephan's good friends.

Heaving heavy breaths, he dropped his feet to the bottom of the pool and shoved the swim goggles on top of his head. Smoothing excess water from his face, he looked up at them.

"Heard you got your heart broken," Reese said.

The closeness of his family was a blessing but at times also a curse. There were very few secrets between them.

"Yeah, what of it?" Still panting, Stephan walked up the stairs and caught the towel Reese threw at him.

Malik sat down in one of the chairs lining the wall. He held a bottle of beer in each hand. "Heard you also risked the payout on your trust fund for some ass. You really take the cake."

"Not just any ass. Ass that Mother warned him away from," Reese said. "Looks like we'll be getting our inheritance around the same time."

Stephan quickly rubbed the towel over his head and body. "I'm glad the two of you are enjoying this so much," he grumbled.

He took one of the bottles from Malik and swallowed a mouthful of beer. Then he plopped down in the chair at a right angle to Malik. Reese remained standing, one hand in his pocket, the other also holding a beer.

"So what happened?" his brother asked.

"We started seeing each other, and it ended," Stephan said with a careless shrug.

"There's more to it than that. I mean, Roselle isn't exactly your type. I was kind of surprised when I heard the two of you were together."

"What's she like?" Malik asked.

"Kinda quiet, keeps to herself mostly, from what I've seen at work."

"She's also smart as hell and has a sense of humor once she opens up. And a smart mouth," Stephan added with a faint smile.

There were times she definitely gave as good as she got, letting him know in a polite but firm way that he was getting out of hand. And thanks to her, he learned to appreciate his blessings and recognize there was more to life than sex and partying.

"So you *like* her like her?" Reese asked.

Stephan scowled at his brother. "What am I, twelve?"

Malik chuckled. "Since you don't want to share your *feelings*, what happened?"

Stephan sighed. "Best I can guess, her great-aunt dying devastated her so much that she wants to be alone now. I don't know. I don't fully understand why she broke up with me, to be honest, but there's nothing I can do about her decision. I don't know how the hell to fix what happened." He took another swig of the beer.

Reese and Malik looked at each other.

"Damn. Sounds like you really care about her," Malik said.

There was silence for a while as Stephan stared at the bottle in his hand. "She's special, no doubt. I liked spending time with her." He shrugged.

Before her, he didn't think about girlfriends, or getting married, and definitely not having a kid. Now, he couldn't stop thinking about getting married and having kids. But not with just anyone. Only with her.

Roselle was that rare combination of sexy and sweet. He was almost certain she had no concept of the appeal she held, which made her dangerous. Women like her snuck up on you, and that's exactly what had happened to him, and he'd fallen in love with her. He couldn't admit that to Malik and Reese yet. His love for her was personal and painfully embarrassing now that she'd ended their relationship.

"Are you sure she ended the relationship for good, or does she need time alone for a while to process what happened?" Malik asked.

"We're done. She won't have anything to do with me," Stephan said with resignation. No point in deluding himself. The finality in her words left no room for optimism that they'd get back together.

Quiet again for a while. Neither Reese nor Malik knew what to say to cheer him up. In all honesty, nothing they said could cheer him up, but having them listen eased the burden of his thoughts.

"Maybe there's nothing you can do about your relationship with her, but you might be able to salvage your screwup with Mother. Have you thought about talking to Father?" Reese asked.

"Yes." He'd considered throwing himself on his father's mercy because he was the only person capable of changing his mother's mind after she'd made a decision. But that meant getting a lecture from his father, and on top of everything else he was going through with Roselle, he wasn't in the mood to hear about all the mistakes he'd made and how he should do better and wasn't living up to his full potential.

"Better swallow that pride, or it'll be another year, maybe two, before you get the money out of that trust."

"Yeah," Stephan said with a resigned sigh. His brother was right, but he simply hadn't been motivated to act.

* * *

"Of all the people to sleep with, you chose one of her most valued employees."

Stephan gritted his teeth, barely refraining from crushing the cup on the table as he sat across from his father, Oscar. He'd taken the morning off to meet him at a local coffee shop. His statement reminded Stephan of why he hadn't wanted to talk to him in the first place.

"You're almost thirty. You need to start acting like an adult and appreciate what you have. There are plenty of people less fortunate."

"I know," Stephan said in an even tone.

He tried to keep the anger out of his eyes as he looked across the table at his father. They had the same fair complexion, but his father's face was round and because of his biracial heritage, had looser curls on his head which he sometimes let grow along with his facial hair, much to his mother's dismay. Sylvie must have recently sent him to the spa because his face was clean-shaven and he had a fresh haircut.

"Do you really know?" Oscar sighed.

"You're not going to believe this, but being with Roselle wasn't about being immature or impulsive. I really care about her or believe me, I wouldn't have risked so much for her."

Oscar's eyes narrowed. "I want to believe you."

"Then believe me."

"Why should I? Based on your track record, all you care about is self-gratification. Why should I convince your mother that this time, you're genuinely sorry and you'll change? Maybe she's right. Maybe you're not ready to handle that kind of money."

"I am ready."

"What have you done to prove it?"

Stephan laughed bitterly and swallowed hard. What he couldn't admit to his brother and cousin yesterday, he was about to admit to his father. Laying bare his feelings, opening up and allowing himself to be vulnerable in front of another person, terrified him. He actually became nauseous, but this was part of being an adult, wasn't it? Doing and saying what made you uncomfortable.

"I've gone in to work every day, on time, I'm learning everything I can, and I'm working on a project to expand Mother's line in Brazil." He sighed. "Aside from that, Roselle consumes me. She is more important to me than any other woman I've ever been involved with. So important that I was willing to risk it all. And I'd do it again. I love her, and if that doesn't prove to you that she's important to me, then I don't know what will."

A frown creased Oscar's brow, and he kept his gaze on Stephan as if trying to figure out if he was being sincere or merely feeding him a line. Stephan understood the skepticism. In the past, he hadn't always been honest. He hadn't always made the right decisions.

He wanted the money, no doubt. But if he had to choose again between his inheritance and being with Roselle, his decision would be the same. He'd pick Roselle every time.

"You really love this woman?" Oscar asked.

"Yes," Stephan replied without hesitation.

Oscar remained quiet, once again staring at his son to determine the truthfulness of his words. "All right, Stephan. I don't think you'd lie about something like that, and I'm sorry the relationship didn't work. Loving someone is one of the highest highs in the world, but when your love isn't reciprocated, it can be one of the lowest lows."

"No kidding. She let me know in no uncertain terms how she feels about me. I want to blame it on her aunt's passing, but I'm not so sure." Stephan turned his cup in a circle on the table.

"Hurt people hurt people. Give her time. She's emotional right now."

"Nah, we're done."

"How can you be done? You said you love her. Listen, your mother and I made the mistake of walking away from each other and not working on our relationship. Big mistake. You and this young woman still have a chance. You had an argument, that's all."

Stephan shook his head. "The difference is, you and mother loved each other, but neither of you would admit it. I love her, but she doesn't care about me. She believes I'm some empty-headed rich jerk without a care in the world."

"You don't know that."

"She told me."

His father didn't have an answer for that.

"I don't want to talk about Roselle anymore. Let's talk about something else."

"All right, about the situation with your inheritance, I'll talk to your mother and see what I can do, but I'm not making any promises."

Stephan let out a relieved breath. "Thanks."

Oscar waved away the appreciation. "Don't thank me yet. I'm not totally convinced I'm doing the right thing. That's her money, not mine. She can do whatever she wants with it, and considering her financial and business acumen is unmatched by anyone else I know, I'm inclined to agree with her decision, but I do sense a change in you. I'll give her my opinion and ask her not to take January first completely off the table, for now. In the coming months, I'd like to see if the changes I'm seeing continue."

"They will. I promise," Stephan said.

Instead of leaving, Stephan and Oscar sat and talked, which included a conversation about Stephan's work at SJ Brands. Oscar quizzed him about the day-to-day business, and he opened up about what he liked and disliked about the job so far. It was the first time in a long time that they'd had a conversation about anything substantive, and Stephan acknowledged this was another missing piece of the puzzle of his life that was getting snapped into place. The father-son relationship had become strained over the years because of him and his personal resentment, but he'd missed the long talks with his father. They'd fallen off after his parents divorced and his father moved to Florida.

Oscar's steady, measured approach to problems was in direct contrast to his mother's kick-down-the-door-and-come-in-with-guns-blazing attitude. Both had their place, and right now, his father's quiet attention and listening ear were what he needed.

They lost track of time, and it was Oscar who finally pointed out how long they'd been sitting there. They scraped back their chairs, tossed the empty beverage cups, and walked out to the parking lot.

Stephan stopped behind his red Ferrari, and Oscar squeezed his shoulder. "Don't make me regret talking to your mother. No more screwups, all right?"

"No more. I promise."

Oscar patted him on the back. "All right. I'll call you soon." He walked away.

"Um, Father."

Oscar turned back around.

"If—if you want to grab coffee again another day, you know… if you're free or something…let me know."

"I'd love that." After pausing for a few seconds, Oscar walked over to Stephan and pulled him into one of his famous bear hugs. Though Stephan's response was less enthusiastic, getting enveloped in his father's embrace was extremely satisfying.

Oscar grinned at him. "I'll call you soon." He strolled off.

Spirits lifted, Stephan climbed into the car and started the engine. A notification on his phone alerted him that he'd received a text. He looked at the screen.

It was a message from Roselle. Seemed his day was getting progressively better. The universe was correcting itself.

Hi. I know it's been a while. Do you mind coming by my place to talk?

Without hesitation, he fired off a response. *I'll be there in 30.*

CHAPTER 25

$\mathcal{H}$e brought flowers.

Stephan stood outside in the hallway, that familiar one-sided smile on his face, but by the time the conversation ended, he'd stop smiling. Perhaps she should have provided more detail in the text, but she hadn't wanted to reveal too much.

"For you." He extended the cluster of red roses.

"Thank you," Roselle murmured.

She took the bouquet and stepped back and let him enter. Her gaze took in the way the gray Henley hugged his broad back and traveled lower to where the jeans fit snug on his behind.

He settled on the sofa in the living room, and she placed the bouquet on the counter in the kitchen, taking that time to harden her resolve. When she came back out, Stephan sat with an ankle resting on his knee, and an arm stretched across the back of the sofa.

"I have to admit, I was surprised to hear from you. You gave me the impression that you and I were over."

Standing several feet away, Roselle rubbed her hands together. "Actually, we are over. Our relationship status hasn't changed."

The contented expression on his face wavered but didn't disappear entirely. "So what did you want to talk to me about?" he asked.

Roselle hesitated. She wasn't sure where to begin.

"What's the matter with you? You're acting nervous, and it's making me nervous," Stephan said with a little laugh.

Roselle took a deep breath. "What I have to tell you is not...you know what, I'm just going to say it. I'm pregnant."

His face blanked. "What?"

"I'm pregnant."

His eyes dropped to her midsection. "Are you absolutely sure?" he asked.

"Positive. I went to the doctor yesterday, and she confirmed that I'm ten weeks pregnant." The doctor had simply verified what she already knew after three positive pregnancy tests.

"Ten weeks? That's around the time the condom broke."

"Yes."

It wasn't unusual for her to have a missed period. Over the years, stress or over-exercising had all caused her to have irregular periods, so when it didn't arrive, she assumed it was her body going through changes. When she missed another one, she suspected there was a problem.

Being ten weeks along meant she hadn't become pregnant in Charlotte when they'd had unprotected sex. Early in their relationship, they'd had an episode when the condom broke. In the back of her mind, she'd known pregnancy was a possibility but hadn't been afraid of the consequences.

Now it was Stephan's turn to stand and appear restless. He paced away from her, rubbing a hand over the back of his head. He stopped in front of the window and stared through the blinds at the building next door. Roselle allowed him time to process the news.

He turned around to look at her. "Are you keeping it?"

"Yes."

"There's a lot we have to consider," he said.

"I realize that we have to break the news to your family, and I'm sure Miss Sylvie won't be pleased."

"That's an understatement. How do you feel?" he asked quietly. "I know that pregnant women go through a lot of changes in their bodies."

Roselle nodded. "There's been a little bit of that. Some soreness in my breasts mostly, but nothing else."

"No nausea or cravings?"

She shook her head. "Not yet. Maybe I'll be one of the lucky ones who doesn't have a lot of symptoms."

"One of my cousins had a lot of problems when she was pregnant with her last baby," he said, obviously trying to make conversation.

Out of compassion, Roselle walked over to him. She ached to touch him but kept her hands to herself. "I don't know what your expectations are, but I'm not trying to trap you."

"What happened was an accident. I don't think that."

"Great, but I had to say it. Of course, I want you to be involved in our child's life, but I'm perfectly capable of taking care of this baby on my own."

He frowned down at her as if she'd grown two more heads.

"I'm not only going to be involved, I'm also going to support you and our child. Listen, you don't fully understand how serious this pregnancy is. We don't only have to break the news to my mother and the rest of the family. Of course, she'll probably be disappointed in both of us, but that's only the beginning. My family has expectations. They're going to expect us to get married."

Whoa. "Married? Why?"

"For appearances, for one. My family on my mother's side is very big on appearances. She's going to expect me to do the right thing."

Roselle couldn't believe she was hearing such an archaic point of view. "The only right thing that you have to do is be in your child's life and help me take care of him or her. Doing the right thing does not mean getting married."

He frowned again. "What's wrong with marrying me?"

He seemed to be offended, but she wanted him to know that she was not interested in a forced marriage. "Nothing is wrong with marrying you, but listen to what you're saying. What's the point of us getting married when we barely know each other?"

"We don't barely know each other," he said, sounding angry now. "We know each other very well. You like chocolate anything —cake, chocolate bars, ice cream. You have a healthy appetite, and you're smart and funny and have an encyclopedia's worth of knowledge in your head about the fashion industry."

"That's all well and good, but that doesn't mean we should get married. We're adults and don't have to do what your family says. I mean, are you seriously considering it?"

He rubbed the back of his neck. "Actually, I am, and I'm having a hard time understanding what your problem is with marrying me."

"Because it's insane! Why in the world would we get married? Marriage is a serious commitment neither of us is ready to make. Certainly not to each other." She turned away from him.

While she was adamant about her decision, she thrilled at the thought of marriage to him and forming a family unit. Something she longed for, considering how her own family had fallen apart with the passing of her father and the rejection of her mother. But she couldn't justify that under the circumstances. If he'd said anything about love, she would have jumped at the chance, but he'd only mentioned marriage because she was pregnant. That simply wasn't good enough.

"Getting married would be a mistake that we'd both regret," she said.

"How are you so sure?"

Roselle turned around to face him. "We'd end up hating each other. Do you really want to bring up a child in a relationship filled with tension and resentment?"

"I want to take care of my kid," Stephan said evenly.

"And you will be able to do that. We can work something out."

"Work something out?" He sounded incredulous. "What are we talking about here? Weekends and holidays?"

"Maybe," she said slowly.

His expression changed into one that she did not recognize. His easygoing face was replaced with one that looked angry but determined. The shift in his demeanor made her very uneasy.

"Hell. No."

"I don't understand what's going on. Marriage is not the only answer," she said.

"Then maybe we're asking the wrong questions. That's my child you're carrying, and I'm a very wealthy man. So rich, that I can't imagine my kid living apart from me and will do everything in my power to make sure that doesn't happen." The level of his voice had elevated—not to the point of yelling, but certainly enough to convey his anger.

"Are you *threatening* me?" Roselle stepped back from him because now she really didn't understand what was going on. Maybe she'd misunderstood his tone and words.

"I'm not making a threat. I'm explaining to you what's going to happen. I'm going to be in my son or daughter's life. Every day. Not weekends, and not holidays. Every. Day."

"Are you planning to live next door to me?" she snapped.

"You're going to move in with me after we get married," he shot back.

She laughed shrilly. "Is this the real Stephan I'm seeing now? The arrogant, rich, entitled man who thinks he can throw his weight and money around and force me into some kind of loveless marriage because I'm pregnant?"

"This isn't a game, Roselle. We're talking about our child here."

"I fully understand that. But we're not only talking about our child, we're talking about our lives as well. One day I might want to date other people. I won't be able to do that if I'm married to you."

He reared back as if she'd swung at him, and his eyebrows lowered over his eyes.

"Everything makes sense now. You really have a problem with me, don't you? You never introduced me to your aunt. You talked about her all the time, but not once did you suggest we meet. I was never really part of your life, was I? You never opened up or shared anything meaningful or real with me about yourself. You always held me at a distance. Don't get too close, Stephan. What were we doing? Just screwing around?"

"*That's what we said,* remember? We had to get the lust out of our system. Well, we did. I did."

"You're really testing my patience right now."

"And you're testing mine. You need to leave. Now."

"I haven't heard your decision yet," he said.

Roselle marched over to the door and swung it open with force. "Then let me be clear. I will not be bullied into making a decision that's not in the best interest of me and my baby. The answer is no." She glared at him.

Stephan marched to the door and stood over her, glowering down into her face with such fury, the heat from his eyes could surely melt metal. She gripped the doorknob, refusing to cower.

"Don't make the mistake of trying to tangle with me," he said in a lethal tone.

Unease trickled down her spine.

"This isn't the Middle Ages. You don't get to club me over the head and haul me off to your tower against my will."

"You're making this harder than it has to be."

"Funny, I was thinking the same thing about you," Roselle said with a defiant tilt to her chin.

"If you think you're going to keep my kid from me—"

"Get out, Stephan. I already said I won't do that, but you don't hear me because you want your way and that's all that matters. You want complete control over me and my child."

"Your child? *Our* child."

Roselle closed her eyes and counted to five. He had literally said *my kid* only two seconds ago but lost his mind when she said something similar.

When she opened her eyes again, Stephan's expression hadn't changed. His cheeks were flushed, and his brown eyes blazed down at her in anger.

"I don't want to talk about this anymore. You're being unreasonable," Roselle said.

"*I'm* being unreasonable? You're talking about our kid as if I'm not a part of its life. You're acting like you don't need shit from me when I know you do. You think my kid is going to live in a two-bedroom apartment when I live in a multimillion-dollar house in one of the most exclusive neighborhoods in Atlanta? Are you out of your fucking mind?"

"You're an asshole!" Roselle yelled at him, standing on her toes.

"That's old news!" he yelled back in her face.

Roselle crossed her arms over her torso. "You don't know if the baby is yours."

Stephan's eyebrows snapped down over his eyes. "What did you say?"

"You heard me."

"So you were screwing around on me?"

"I didn't say that."

"So what do you mean?"

"You want to get married, and you don't know if this is your baby!" The exclamation dropped like a bomb in the middle of the room.

Both of them stared at each other, and she immediately regretted the words.

There was no point in going down that road. The child was his, no question, and her ridiculous attempt to derail the conversation would only create more problems.

"Forget it. I want you to go. Your reaction is way over the top, and I can't deal with you right now."

He pointed a finger in her face. "I advise you to think long and hard about what you're doing and come to the right decision. You don't want to deal with the consequences."

"Marry you or else? That's such a sweet offer, but I'll pass. You think because I don't have anyone you can push me around and force me to do whatever you want? You can't." Her voice wobbled as tears filled her throat. "I'm strong all on my own. I don't need you. I don't need anybody!"

Emotion flickered across Stephan's face. He looked away from her, his jaw tight. "You'll be hearing from me."

He strode into the hallway and Roselle slammed the door shut and locked it. Trembling, she rested her forehead against the cool wood and took in a shaky breath.

That did not go at all how she'd planned. Even worse, she didn't know what Stephan's threat meant. Maybe he simply needed to cool down.

She went into the living room and sank onto the sofa. The faint scent of his cologne lingered in the room, and her throat tightened in misery.

She buried her face in her hands and squeezed her eyes shut. A few tears escaped, and she angrily wiped them away.

Once he calmed down, everything would be okay. At least that's what she hoped. But she had a funny feeling, there were worse things to come.

CHAPTER 26

*T*revor, his parents' housekeeper, led Stephan into the sitting room. The older man's uniform consisted of a gray top and gray pants. The hair on his head was also gray. He'd worked for his mother for years and ran her household according to her very precise instructions.

The room was decorated in a neutral palette of alabaster and dove gray, with two loveseats and a chaise lounge in front of the fireplace. A photo of Sylvie in between her two brothers—holding onto Cyrus's arm and her head resting on Anthony's arm—sat on a side table in a silver frame. All three of them were dressed in evening attire and smiling into the camera.

Outside on the balcony, his parents wore loose-fitting shirts and pants as they mimicked the movements of their tai chi instructor, a tall, slender Asian woman.

"They should be finishing up soon. Can I get you anything to drink?" Trevor asked.

"No, I'm good. Thanks." Stephan sat on one of the loveseats and prepared for his parents' wrath.

Trevor reentered the room with four glasses of water on a tray and quietly left again. Though he'd said he didn't want anything, Stephan was glad he'd brought in the water after all. He lifted one of the glasses and took a sip, waiting patiently for his parents to finish their exercise.

He didn't have to wait long. A few minutes later, the session wrapped up, and all three of them entered the room.

"Stephan, darling. I didn't know you were here. Have you been waiting long?" Sylvie asked.

"Not too long," he replied.

"You remember Annie, don't you?" Sylvie picked up one of the glasses.

Stephan stood. "I do. Nice to see you again." He shook the instructor's hand.

"Good to see you again, Stephan," Annie said. She drank half her water, and after a brief conversation with his parents about the next session, she left them alone.

"To what do we owe this visit?" Oscar sat down across from Stephan and sipped his water.

Stephan sat down, too. He'd worked out the conversation in his head on the way over, but no matter how he broke the news, his parents, particularly his mother, would be furious. But he wanted a role in his child's life, no matter how much the prospect of being a father unnerved him. He had some doubts—after all, babies didn't come with a manual, but he knew he would be a good father.

"I came to give you both some news. You're going to be grand-parents again."

"Excuse me, what was that?" Oscar looked profoundly confused.

"We know we're about to become grandparents again. Simone's baby boy is due in October—only six more weeks." Sylvie spoke slowly and then took a sip of water.

"I was talking about me," Stephan said, eyeing his mother.

Her eyes hardened, and she carefully set the glass of water back on the tray in front of him. "You're not married," she said calmly.

"I know that."

They stared at each other, and tension thickened the air.

177

Oscar leaned forward. "Stephan, how did this...never mind. Who is the mother and how far along is she?"

"Roselle, and she's ten weeks pregnant."

"Roselle, my employee?" Sylvie looked at Oscar but pointed at Stephan. "You see what has happened? And you want me to change my mind about the trust. Why? Look at the mess he's made yet again."

Stephan took the tongue-lashing.

Oscar kept his gaze on Stephan. "I'm sure he's remorseful."

"Remorseful is not enough! His behavior must change, and it has not. Instead of getting better, it's become progressively worse. Now he's gotten Roselle—my employee—pregnant. And you want me to go easy on him? I will not. I have indulged his behavior long enough. No more."

It was strange to hear the parental roles had reversed, with his father being his champion while his mother insisted on meting out punishment.

Sylvie swung a fierce look in Stephan's direction. "Did you explain to her that you're getting married?"

"Sylvie," Oscar said in a warning voice.

"No, Oscar. He will do the right thing and marry her. He will be responsible."

"She doesn't want to marry me."

"Did you ask her?" Sylvie demanded.

"Of course. She doesn't want to marry me, and she doesn't have to." No matter how much he wanted her to. No matter how much, in retrospect, he'd seen her pregnancy as an opportunity to lock her down and had simply used his mother as an excuse.

"Of course she has to marry you. For heaven's sake, why wouldn't she? You can support her and my grandchild, and it's the right thing to do. You will not be an absentee father."

Oscar slammed his glass on the table, and both Sylvie and Stephan swung their heads in his direction. "Sylvie, you can't force them to get married. You're being ridiculous."

"How am I being ridiculous? You forbade me to interfere

because you said that he loves her and was heartbroken over their split. Do you love her, Stephan?"

"Yes."

"Does she love you?"

Pain wrenched through him. "No."

"*No?*" Sylvie repeated, incredulous. "Why not?"

There was a shift in the conversation. Sylvie had pivoted into protective mode. Minutes ago she'd complained about Stephan's behavior, but now she couldn't fathom why anyone wouldn't adore him.

"We're not compatible."

"You were compatible enough to sleep with and create a child with."

Stephan ran a hand down the back of his head and sat back. "She made it clear what she thinks about me, and marriage is off the table."

Sylvie placed her hands on her hips. "Indeed? Well, marriage may be off the table, but making sure you have access to your child is not. I will handle this. I'll make an appointment for you and me with the attorneys next week. We will discuss options on how to proceed. I will also contact HR first thing on Monday because there is no way she will continue to work at my company while she keeps me from my grandbaby."

Sylvie was ready for war, as surely as if she'd donned camouflage gear and makeup. She stormed out, and silence filled the room, out of place after her explosive rant.

"Well, that went well." Oscar sighed. "I thought I told you nothing else."

"Guess I didn't listen, as usual."

"I don't think I can talk your mother down this time."

"I don't want you to talk her down."

"Why not? You understand she's about to unleash hell on Roselle."

"I'm fine with that."

"Why?"

"Because I want my kid. Because I don't want to be an absentee father who sees my kid a few days at a time or a couple weekends out of the year. Maybe less if Roselle ever moves away from Atlanta."

Oscar sat forward. "If that comment was directed at me, I tried. But as you got older, you kids didn't want to spend as much time with me. You preferred to go on lavish vacations and party and spend time with your celebrity friends."

"Kind of like you preferred spending time on your boat with all of your young hot girlfriends."

"There weren't that many," Oscar said through clenched teeth.

If there was one thing his father hated, it was anyone referencing the younger women he became involved with during the period he and Sylvie were divorced.

Stephan didn't want to fight with his father. They were in a good place now. "To be honest, none of that matters. It's in the past. All I know is, I'm waking up with my kid in the morning and putting them to bed at night. That's what I want, and if Mother can make that happen, so be it. She's angry at me, but we both want the same outcome, which is my son or my daughter with me every day."

"Think about what you're doing. You have your mother and your whole family and soon a team of attorneys. Who does Roselle have?"

He'd never had to be responsible for anything in his life. Never had to do the right thing. And now, the one time—the one time he tried to be responsible and do the right thing, he wasn't allowed to. Well, Roselle would have to deal with the consequences.

Hardening his heart, Stephan stood. "She should've thought of that before she tossed my proposal back in my face."

He walked out without another word.

CHAPTER 27

"*D*id you come in here to rant, or did you want advice?" Ella asked.

"Both," Stephan answered wearily. He stood in Ella's gourmet kitchen, bitching and complaining about his situation.

He watched her cut the crust off peanut butter and jelly sandwiches for Hannah and Sophia, who at the moment were running around in the backyard with their black lab, Scruffy.

"If it were me, no way I'm giving up my baby," his other sister Simone said, rubbing her belly. She and her husband lived next door.

She sat in a cushioned armchair Tyrone and Stephan had carted into the large kitchen for her comfort. She looked ready to have her baby at any moment. Yet she'd waltzed into the house with her chestnut skin glowing, wearing a designer dress and a pair of heels that seemed precariously high considering her condition. That was Simone, though. She was glamorous and looked her best at all times.

"I didn't ask her to give up the baby. I asked her to marry me," Stephan said.

"Since the ranting part of the conversation is over, I'll give you my advice. I have a theory," Ella said.

"What's your theory?"

Ella set down the knife. "She's doing what she thinks Mother would do."

His brow furrowed. "What does our mother have to do with anything?"

"Think about how much she admires our mother."

He shrugged. "So what? Lots of people admire Mother, and fear her, too."

Ella nodded her head. "I understand that, but my point is, she admired Mother for a very long time. A few years ago, Roselle went through a period where she wasn't taking care of herself. Mother gave her a complete makeover—new haircut, new wardrobe, all of which probably made quite an impression on her. She's also taken her under her wing to offer further development. Roselle probably felt guilty about sleeping with you because of her relationship with Mother and worried it could affect their relationship. Of course, when she found out she was pregnant, she must've panicked at first. But when you told her you'd have to get married—which isn't exactly a proposal, by the way—she decided that it wasn't the best decision for you, her, and the baby."

"Well, she's wrong," Stephan said with vehemence.

"Says you," Simone chimed in.

"The point is," Ella continued, "she's doing whatever she has to do to protect her family unit. And her family unit is her and that baby."

Stephan silently considered his sister's words. "She's being strong, protecting the family unit, the same way Mother would."

"Exactly. She's doing what she thinks her mentor would do. She's fighting back. She feels intimidated and is standing her ground. She's in a delicate place right now, excited about having the baby but having no one to share the excitement with."

"But it's my kid, too!"

"I know, and I'm sympathetic, but she needs support, not aggression. Whatever you decide, you know I have your back. We all do, but you have to do the right thing."

"She's right," Simone interjected. "The last thing Roselle needs right now is a fight on her hands, and right on the cusp of her aunt dying, too."

Stephan cringed inwardly. He'd thought about that. He didn't want to cause Roselle any more grief, but the selfishness in him found it hard to let go and wanted to force her hand. If it were possible to marry her tomorrow, he'd do it.

"I want her," he said thickly. "This isn't just about the baby. I want *her*. I want the three of us to be a family."

Ella's tone gentled. "You may not get that, and you could choose to forego what you want. To be selfless. To do the right thing for her. I know you love her and the baby. But you can't get what you want this time. So how are you going to handle it? Mother is ready to go full throttle this week. Is that what you want? I don't think so. If you want Roselle to stop pushing back against you, you have to make her feel safe. I bet if she feels safe, doesn't believe she's being pushed around, she won't fight you anymore."

"Make her feel safe," Stephan repeated.

He could do that, but before he reached out to Roselle again, he wanted to find out more about her past. What had she withheld from him that could help him understand her better?

* * *

THE CORDOBA AGENCY was a private security firm that offered protection and other "services" to wealthy clients. They were known for their discretion and stellar work, which was well worth their hefty fees.

The entire operation was owned by Cruz Cordoba, a big Cuban standing at about six feet five and looking like he could crush small cars between his forearm and biceps.

After being ushered into Cruz's office, Stephan sat down in front of his desk, and Cruz slid a black folder toward him.

"It's not pretty," he said solemnly. "She was raped at sixteen by a guy named Charles Baker. Tied her to the bed and assaulted her multiple times over several hours. The ties left marks on her wrists."

Sickened by the words, Stephan's right hand clenched into a fist. "Where is Charles Baker now?" He'd rip him limb from limb.

"I know what you're thinking, but somebody already beat you to it."

"Who? Some other guy who's woman he raped?"

"His wife. Gutted him after he raped her."

Startled by the revelation, Stephan was unable to speak for a few moments. "He raped his wife?"

"It happens. There was a trial that took place three years ago. According to testimony, the wife—Cheryl—after she found out Charles had been cheating on her with a coworker, told him she intended to leave him and take the kids with her. The marriage had been deteriorating for years anyway, so she wasn't broken up about it. When she told him her plans, he assaulted her that night. It wasn't the first time during their five years together. If you read the details, you'll see she learned to appease him. She'd also evidently expected a problem because she'd sent the kids to stay with her parents overnight."

"Damn."

Stephan knew marital rape existed, but what kind of monster forced himself on any woman, much less his own wife, the woman he'd vowed to love and cherish? He flipped open the folder while Cruz continued with his commentary.

"The DA tried to say the murder was premeditated because Cheryl made sure the kids were out of the house, but her parents were well off and hired a great attorney. She also had photos of bruises on her wrists from that night and a few other times when he'd assaulted her."

"Son of a bitch never changed his tactics," Stephan said bitterly.

"The defense had several witnesses take the stand to show a pattern of behavior. Understandably, not all of them came forward. Roselle did."

What must she have gone through, having to relive that trauma?

"When did you say this happened?" Stephan paused on a grisly photo of the crime scene. Charles' wife had done a number on the son of a bitch, but no more than he deserved after hurting so many women.

"Three years ago."

That had to be around the time Ella said Roselle wasn't taking care of herself.

Stephan set the folder on the table and ran a hand over the back of his head. He had a lot to digest. "What happened to the wife?"

"She was found not guilty."

"A happy ending of sorts," Stephan muttered.

"There's something else you should know," Cruz said.

Stephen braced for more bad news.

"Charles Baker was a hotshot basketball player, the kind of guy with a promising career that people in a small town don't want to see derailed. Your girlfriend was basically ostracized by the good town folk. Her friends eventually turned their backs on her, and her own mother..." Cruz shook his head. "Her own mother didn't stick up for her. Called her fast, said she had no business sneaking out and going over to Charles' house. Basically, posing the same questions we've heard a million times. *What did she think would happen when she went up to his bedroom?* Eventually, she sent her here to live with her great aunt. Sending her away served two purposes. She didn't have to answer for her daughter's accusations, and Charles Baker could go on with his life."

"Man." Sickened, Stephan ran a hand down his face and sat for a moment and digested everything Cruz had told him. Finally, he stood and picked up the folder, though he wasn't sure he would ever read through it in detail. He'd heard enough. He shook Cruz's hand. "Thanks, this was very helpful."

"Sure thing. I have a question for you though—what would you have done if he was alive and you'd caught up with Charles?" Cruz asked, eyes narrowed.

Stephan paused. "Probably something to get my ass in trouble. But now we'll never know."

He left the building with Roselle on the brain. No wonder she felt alone. No wonder she was adamant about standing up for herself because other than her great aunt, history had taught her not to count on others for help. Not friends. Not family. She'd been traumatized again after being traumatized by that monster.

Right then he vowed he'd do whatever was necessary to make sure Roselle never felt alone again.

* * *

Sylvie's sitting room was deathly quiet. Seconds before, Stephan told his mother he no longer wanted to pursue legal action against Roselle.

"I beg your pardon? Brit has already sent papers to inform her that you will pursue full custody of the baby once it is born. You are in a much better financial position to take care of the child. You have plenty of space for a child to run around and play in. You have the support of your entire family and me. Roselle doesn't even have a job. Before I had the chance to contact HR, she sneaked into the office on Sunday, cleared out the personal belongings from her office, and sent me a rather cryptic resignation—effective immediately." Sylvie's lips tightened with displeasure.

"Mother, I want you to stop. Leave her alone. She didn't do anything wrong. She's not hurting me. I'm hurting her by taking legal action against her." Stephan swallowed. "She's being strong, like you. And I admire her for it."

"Are you trying to sweet-talk me?"

"No, I mean it. I do admire you. And I love you. If you love me as much as you say you do, you'll respect my wishes. Don't interfere. Don't hurt her. I...I want to protect her. Take care of her. Even if I can't have my way." He took a deep breath. "I hired the Cordoba Agency to look into her background. She was sexually assaulted at sixteen."

Sylvie's hand flew to her mouth. "Oh, no. Who did that to her?"

"A guy from back in her home town. A hotshot basketball player who everyone was concerned about. Very few were concerned about Roselle." He gave her a summary of what he'd discussed with Cruz. "That's why I want you to stop, and under no circumstances are you to use this information against her."

"Good heavens, Stephan, of course I won't use it against her. I'm your mother, not the evil villain in a superhero movie."

Stephan almost smiled.

"You said the trial took place three years ago? She changed around that time. She was one of my in-house designers, and I noticed she'd become horribly thin and clearly wasn't taking care of herself. That must have been around the time of the trial. That poor girl." Sylvie's fingers encircled her throat. "I will call off the lawyers. I assume you're going to talk to Roselle?"

Stephan nodded. "I'm not sure what we'll be able to work out, but we'll figure it out."

Sylvie took his hand and squeezed it. "You will, and I will stay out of it, and let you figure out your next steps. My only request is that I have access to my grandchild."

"I'll be sure to include that in the negotiations," Stephan said with amusement.

Sylvie's sympathetic gaze swept his features. "I'm sorry your relationship didn't last."

"I thought you didn't like us together."

"I didn't. Workplace relationships are notoriously problematic, and as I mentioned to you, I didn't want to lose her as an employee. Yet, here we are." She stared at him accusingly, and Stephan smothered a sigh. "But I've been thinking about the two of you the past few days, and in conversation with your father, we think you and Roselle are well-matched."

"Roselle doesn't think so."

"Well, she's missing out on a good husband, and I know you'll be an excellent father."

"Really?" Doubts plagued him, though the prospect of becoming a father excited him.

"I raised you, darling. Of course you will be." She patted his hand, but then a frown wrinkled her brow. "Though at times, I wonder if I failed you. Maybe if I'd been stricter, like your father suggested…" She shook her head, frowning in consternation.

"You didn't fail. Thank you for always being there, during the good times and the bad. Thank you for never turning your back on me during my fu—screwups. Everything you did, I appreciate. I didn't appreciate what I had before, but I do now. Unconditional love—that's what you've always given us. Yes, sometimes you stifle us." She arched a brow, and he laughed at her expression. "But I know everything you do comes from a good place. A place of love. And…" His voice thickened as he thought of the rejection Roselle and others like her faced from people who should protect them and have their back. "I no longer take you for granted. You helped shape me into the man I am today. Thank you, Mother."

The corners of her eyes crinkled into a smile, and she cupped his cheek. "I love you, my darling."

"I love you, too."

CHAPTER 28

*S*tephan stared up at the ceiling. "I have to go to work."

"Work?" the brunette beside him repeated.

"Yeah. I work now." He rolled out of bed in a pair of boxers and ran a palm over the stubble on his jaw.

"Since when?"

Continuing toward the bathroom, he didn't answer. He wasn't in the mood to have a conversation.

They didn't have sex last night, though it wasn't for lack of trying. He'd convinced himself that he should go back to life before Roselle. Why tie his peace of mind to one woman when so many others were available?

He'd enjoyed Lara before, and that's why he'd invited her over after the birthday dinner at his parents' penthouse. But his penis refused to cooperate. Roselle had control of his mind, heart, and body. How long was this going to continue? He hadn't been with a woman since they last made love, and that was two months ago! His longest drought on record.

He stared at his image, but his vision became clouded by thoughts of bouncy, shoulder-length hair and expressive eyes. Of Roselle licking Nutella from the corner of her mouth, as they walked along the streets of Paris. Of eating a chocolate torte in a semi-lit bakery, and then running in the rain back to their apartment and making love—their damp bodies sliding together in the soft sheets.

Yesterday was his birthday, and for the first time in years, he hadn't thrown a party. He'd received dozens of calls and texts beforehand to find out the location of the party, and on his birthday to wish him a happy thirtieth. His Instagram page had been inundated with best wishes from strangers and celebrity acquaintances.

Despite all that, he opted to spend a quiet evening with family. Sylvie, because she'd promised not to interfere, wanted to fix one of his problems, and arranging the dinner was her way of doing something to make him feel better. So he'd accepted her invitation for dinner with the immediate family and their spouses.

There were moments during the celebration when Roselle entered his thoughts. For instance, when Trevor brought out a big cake with lit candles in the shape of the number thirty, which Sophia and Hannah helped him blow out. That moment reminded him of Roselle's birthday in Paris and how pleased she'd been with the chocolate cake. And how good he'd felt making her happy.

He put toothpaste on his brush.

He hadn't spoken to her yet. The day after he and his mother talked, he left a voicemail letting her know they'd called off the attorneys. An hour later, he received a text.

Thank you.

That was it. Nothing else. She never asked how he was doing. She didn't suggest they get together and synchronize their calendars around her appointments. But why would she? He was the idiot who thought they'd had something special. He'd cared too much and made the ultimate mistake. He'd fallen in love with her.

When she broke up with him, she took a chunk of his heart, leaving only enough for him to survive. And that's what he'd do.

Survive. He and Roselle were not going to be in a romantic relationship, so moving forward, his primary focus was his child.

They needed to talk about co-parenting, but until then, he had to go to work.

* * *

HE DIDN'T GO to work.

Stephan called in sick, went to Roselle's building, and sat outside her apartment in the hallway. He knocked earlier, but she didn't open the door. He called, but there was no answer. So he decided to wait. Every now and again, he stood and walked around, stretching his legs and making sure his butt didn't go numb on the hard floor. Otherwise, he remained in place. She had to leave sometime.

The elevator pinged in the distance, and his head swung to the right to see who was coming. Kay, Roselle's roommate, came down the hall with the handle of a paper sack in each hand. She wasn't traveling this week, and they'd seen each other earlier when she left to go to the grocery store.

"You're still here?" Kay wore glasses, and her dirty blonde hair was cut in a page boy style with long bangs that touched her lashes.

"I told you I wasn't going anywhere." He talked a good game, but pretty soon his bladder might force him to leave, if only for a few minutes.

"She doesn't want to talk to you."

Stephan stood. "You need help with those bags?"

She shook her head. "You're insane."

He shrugged. "I've been told."

Kay set the bags on the floor. She opened the door and paused before closing it. "I'll let her know you're out here." She actually seemed sympathetic.

"Thanks." He doubted it would make a difference, but it couldn't hurt to be hopeful.

Stephan shoved his hands in his pockets and leaned back against the wall, resting his head and closing his eyes. Five minutes later, the door opened.

His heart leaped in his chest. He hadn't seen Roselle since September. She had a baby bump, made obvious by the way the white T-shirt hugged her middle.

"Hey," she said.

"Hey." He was so relieved that she was speaking to him, he didn't move.

"I wasn't sure about talking to you. Those documents I received from your attorney were pretty scary."

They were supposed to be scary and overwhelming to frighten her into changing her mind. "I know, but I promise that's all over and done with."

She gnawed the side of her mouth. "You want to come in?"

He swallowed. "Yeah."

Roselle let Stephan inside and led him back to her bedroom since Kay was in the kitchen unpacking groceries and might over-hear them if they remained in the living room.

Back to the dresser, she stood with her hands clasped before her. Her eyes ate him up after they'd been apart for so long. He knew how to command a room. Feet apart, he wore a black jacket and white shirt underneath and the ever-present Vacheron Constantin timepiece on his wrist—the type of clothing he typi-cally wore to work.

"Happy belated birthday," she said.

His eyebrows raised as if he were surprised she knew about it. She'd peeped at his Instagram account a couple of days ago and seen where people were asking about plans for his birthday party, but he never responded.

"Thanks." He rubbed his hands together. "I don't want to take up a lot of your time. I came by to make you a revised offer. Forget about getting married. I thought about a compromise where you can get the support you need, and I can be close to the baby in this process."

"I'm listening," Roselle said quietly, warily.

"I want you to move in with me." He lifted a palm toward her. "Before you protest, hear me out. There's plenty of space at the house, and I already talked to Reese, and he doesn't mind. No one would bother you, and you'd have your own bedroom and bathroom. No strings, no requirements, except to keep me up-to-date on what's happening with your appointments and the health of our baby."

"That's very unconventional. Won't that put a cramp in your dating life?"

"My dating life is nonexistent right now, and besides, I'm more concerned about making sure you're okay, and you deliver a healthy baby."

Still no mention of love for her, but it was clear he loved their unborn child already. She'd be greedy to ask for more, and the truth was, she was running out of money and hadn't been able to find work—part-time or full-time—since she left SJ Brands. She'd be in real trouble soon. No one wanted to hire a visibly pregnant woman.

Roselle stared down at her fingers. Could she handle living in such close proximity to Stephan and not be able to touch him, the way she ached to do right now? Not have him touch her?

She'd been scared to death when she received those papers from the attorney's office that threatened to take her baby, wondering where she could find a lawyer with the experience and skill Stephan's family easily afforded, to fight them on equal footing.

At times, when loneliness overwhelmed her, she felt as if she were coming apart at the seams. Kay was nice, but they weren't that close. She wished she had someone to talk to. She lacked peace of mind because she had no one to share her deepest fears with.

She had to hold it together. If not for herself, for the baby she carried.

"I know what happened to you at sixteen."

Roselle's head snapped up. "What did you say?" His words reverberated like sound waves inside her chest.

Compassion filled his eyes. "I know what happened, and I know you had to relive the ordeal three years ago when you testified on behalf of his widow."

Her fingers tightened around each other. "You researched my background?" she asked in a hoarse whisper.

"I wanted to understand you."

What did he think of her now? Roselle closed her arms around her torso and lowered her gaze, steeling herself for the blow of condemnation. If he judged her, too, she would fall apart.

"What happened to you was terrible. That guy was a piece of shit." He spoke with such bitterness in his voice, she lifted her gaze.

He didn't blame her, but she saw pity in his eyes. "So now you feel sorry for me."

"Yes, I do feel sorry for you. I won't apologize for caring. No one should have to go through what you did or the aftermath when the people you knew turned their backs on you because they didn't believe you or because they blamed you for your own attack. I wanted… I wanted to kill that guy, but he's already dead." His right hand had curled into a fist, ready to strike out at the invisible danger.

Charles was long gone, but the demons from that night never completely left. She longed to rush into Stephan's arms and get the comfort she craved but pressed her back against the dresser to fight the urge.

"How long can I stay at your house?"

"As long as you want."

"What about Kay? I have to give her notice. I can't abandon her."

"I'll take care of whatever you owe her and make sure she's set for a few months until she finds a new roommate. What else?"

The urge to run into his arms again overwhelmed her, but the distance between them precluded that. It was—figuratively and might as well be physically—as wide as the Atlantic Ocean.

"I guess there's nothing else. I accept your revised offer," she said softly.

CHAPTER 29

"*We* did it!" Marcus exclaimed. He looked like he'd won the lottery.

Stephan touched his glass against Marcus's and Jayson's glasses as they sat around a table on the company's private jet. After months of research, long-distance conversations, and visits to São Paulo, they signed a distribution deal with a Brazilian chain hours earlier. All their hard work had finally paid off.

Marcus let Stephan take the lead on the project, and Stephan pulled in Jayson. They'd developed a great work relationship. Jayson was an asset to the team and quite smart once he dialed back the eagerness and inappropriate comments.

Stephan let the cool champagne wash down his throat. Stretching his legs, he loosened his tie and glanced out the window.

A lot had happened in the past four months, with time skipping along quickly and one day running into the next. Trenton and Alannah had a baby boy in December, and Simone had delivered a healthy baby boy back in October and had taken time off from her work for the family's foundation to be with her newborn.

He had received his inheritance on January first without

fanfare, and Reese had moved out of the house, stating it was time for him to get his own place. Meanwhile, Malik and his fiancée Lindsay were in the midst of planning a wedding. SJ Brands signed a deal with Rue de la Mode and work had already begun on the designs.

The living situation between him and Roselle was still problematic. They stayed in the same house but lived somewhat separate lives, managing to be cordial and friendly when they ran into each other or ate a meal together. Roselle let him know about checkups and anything concerning the baby. Otherwise, they kept their interactions to a minimum.

He offered to hire a decorator for the nursery, but she preferred to design the room herself and had already changed her mind several times because she wanted everything to be perfect. The white walls had at first been painted pastel green, but now they were pale yellow. Her latest project was stenciling jungle animals onto the walls.

The stress of remaining on the periphery and keeping his distance had taken a toll. He didn't get much sleep nowadays when the woman he loved was right down the hall, and the pending birth of his first child made him second-guess the type of father he'd be. He'd only recently started being responsible and taking care of himself. How was he supposed to take care of a completely helpless human being who depended on him?

"You have big plans when you get back?" Marcus asked.

"Nothing but rest and relaxation," Stephan answered.

"Same. The past few days have been exhausting, but it was all worth it," Jayson said.

"Everything else okay?" Marcus asked.

"Everything else is fine," Stephan answered.

People at work knew he and Roselle were having a baby together and that she'd moved in with him, but they never came right out and said her name or asked specifically unless he broached the subject. It was comical the way they tiptoed around the topic. He learned Inez was the person who had tipped off his mother about eating lunch with Roselle and their affair months ago, but he didn't think she was the leak to staff about the baby and their living arrangements. She was way too loyal to his mother to disclose that news. It was simply information that managed to become known somehow.

Online, rumors were floating around that he'd gotten someone pregnant, but no one knew for sure, and since he didn't post about it or respond to questions on his social media, the rumors didn't generate enough interest for anyone to do further digging. That was fine with him. He'd seen what happened when his cousin Gavin's girlfriend had become pregnant with twins. Gavin had a much larger social media presence than Stephan, and people had been ruthless, calling his woman all kinds of names and accusing her of trapping him. He wanted to avoid the same catastrophe with Roselle.

"Well, fellas, I'm going to get some rest. Wake me up when we land." Marcus drained his glass and then went to lie down on the sofa. Within minutes, his snores filled the cabin. Jayson reclined his chair and started reading on his tablet, which meant Stephan was on his own for entertainment for the next nine hours.

He removed his phone from his pocket and thumbed through the photo gallery. He stopped at a photo of Roselle asleep on one of the high-backed chairs in the theater room. Her lips were slightly parted, and both hands rested on her belly. She always fell asleep watching movies, if not during the first, definitely by the second. He'd taken the photo on impulse, to tease her about it and provide evidence to her denials that she fell asleep during movies. But then he remembered they didn't have that kind of playful relationship anymore. So he simply looked at it and wished their relationship was different.

* * *

STEPHAN WALKED INTO THE KITCHEN. Paula, his house manager, was in there wiping down one of the counters. She was an older white woman with wrinkles around her eyes and a long gray braid that landed in her lower back.

She turned at the sound of him setting his briefcase and jacket on the counter.

"Hi, Stephan, are you hungry?"

"Not really. I might eat a couple of pieces of toast or something and then head upstairs."

"The maid service will be late next week, and the nutritionist wanted me to ask you one more time if you're sure you don't want her to recommend some keto meals to you."

"What is it with her and the keto diet? I'm not interested. Ask if she's sure she wants to continue being my nutritionist and see what she says." Stephan pulled open the refrigerator door.

"What are you looking for?"

"Peach jam. Are we out?"

Paula walked over to the cabinet and took down a fresh jar of his favorite peach jam.

He stared at her in disbelief. "Paula, you like me." Every time she wanted to punish him, she'd "forget" his jam.

"Don't get carried away. I only bought it because your wife reminded me and I want to make a good impression on her." She walked past him toward the door.

"I don't have a wife, Paula," he said.

"Not yet," she called back.

He shook his head. She continued to predict that he and Roselle would get married. Based on what, he had no idea. She never saw them being affectionate. They were more like acquaintances than former lovers.

He made the toast and slathered each side with butter and jam. Seated at the island, he ate his midnight snack and sipped a beer. A smile spread across his face when a message popped up on his phone from Sylvie. A big deal since she seldom texted.

Great job in Brazil. Very proud of you.

As he continued to sip the IPA, he simultaneously sorted emails, deleting unneeded ones and bookmarking others.

Then a sound at the kitchen entrance captured his attention.

Roselle stood in the doorway in white and blue striped shorts and the matching nightshirt that looked two sizes too small because of how it stretched across her very large stomach. She'd brushed her hair into a topknot and was barefoot and didn't have on a stitch of makeup on her fuller face.

Her cinnamon-brown skin glowed, giving her an angelic appearance, but his thoughts were far from holy when he noticed the tops of her breasts were visible at the neckline where she'd undone one of the buttons. His pants tightened in the crotch area, which always seemed to happen at the most inopportune times. He wanted to go straight to bed, but he'd have to rub one out in the shower. Maybe that would help him sleep tonight.

"You're back," Roselle said.

"Came in a few minutes ago."

"How did it go?"

"They signed with us."

"Stephan, that's great! Congratulations."

The pride in her voice made him sit up taller. He'd proved, not only to himself but to everyone else, that he was more than a pretty face. "Thanks. Couldn't have done it without you."

"That's not true. You'd have found a way to pull together the information you needed. Besides, you were the salesman. I had nothing to do with that."

"Thanks anyway," he said, watching her waddle over to the refrigerator. So cute.

His gaze zeroed in on the exposed back of her neck. He would kill for a chance to kiss that spot and listen to her breathy pleas as she wiggled her soft ass against him. Then he'd enter her from behind. He loved to hear the soft little sounds she made when he hit it just right.

Thoughts like that were no good. He drained half his beer. "What are you doing up so late?"

"The baby won't let me sleep. She's very active tonight, moving around a lot."

They were having a girl but hadn't decided on a name yet.

"Your mother came by today. Your father came with her this time, and they brought more gifts."

"Again?"

Roselle nodded and laughed. "She informed me her grandchild will want for nothing. She brought up the baby shower again, but I told her I don't see the point. You're still okay we didn't have one, right?"

"Definitely. We don't have to have a shower you don't want. We can get everything she needs ourselves. And obviously, that's not an issue, because my family will make sure we have more than enough."

"I know family members and friends like to be involved, and I get the impression your family definitely wants to be involved."

"They'll be fine, trust me. Our baby is the most important thing right now."

She seemed satisfied with the answer. She poured a glass of water, drank it, and set the empty glass in the sink.

"Okay. Good night, then."

"Good night," he said.

She walked away, and the ache in his loins magnified the farther she walked away from him.

Roselle paused at the doorway with a hand on her belly. She turned. "She's at it again. Want to feel?"

The question took him aback. She'd never offered to let him feel the baby move before.

"Yeah." For some reason, his hands suddenly became clammy. He was about to make a small connection with his unborn child, which he hadn't done before.

Roselle came to stand in front of him and unbuttoned the lower buttons of the shirt to show her stretched belly. He saw what looked like a finger poking under her skin.

"Holy crap. Did that hurt?" he whispered.

"It feels weird, but it doesn't hurt, except when she pokes me in the navel or kicks me in the kidneys." She laughed softly.

She took his hand and placed it on her belly. His daughter's movements tickled his palm. He was so moved by the experience, he bent his head closer to Roselle's belly. "Hey in there. What are you doing to Mommy? Settle down."

Instead of settling down, his daughter's movements increased.

Eyes bright, Roselle laughed at her agitation. "Now she's really moving around. She must like the sound of your voice."

Stephan continued talking to his daughter until she settled down. "She's finally going to sleep. Maybe now you can get some rest." In case his daughter moved again, he didn't remove his hands, but also because he was finally making skin-to-skin contact with Roselle in a meaningful way.

Occasionally, they'd brushed against each other, or he'd held her arm as he helped her out of the car on the way to an appointment. But this, this was much more intimate. Watching his fingers spread out over her taut belly stirred his blood.

Roselle placed a hand to the back of his head and let it trail down to his jaw. Her gentle touch sent shivers down his spine. He looked up and saw tears in her eyes.

"I never said you were shallow," she said in a thick voice.

"Not in so many words, but that's what you meant." Fatigue burned the back of his eyes. He didn't want to have this conversation now. They were way past that argument from months ago.

"I was emotional."

"Maybe you said what you were really thinking."

"*No*," she said with quiet intensity. "I was scared."

"Of what?"

Her lower lip trembled. "That you'd leave me, too. I don't have anybody. Only my baby."

He kissed the palm of her hand and then looked into her expressive brown eyes. "You have me. I keep telling you that, but you don't hear me. I'm not going anywhere. I love you."

She blinked. "What?"

Goddammit. His gut wrenched at the slipup.

"I've said too much." He started to rise.

"No, no, wait." Roselle pressed her hands on his thighs and forced him to stay in place. "Why didn't you say something before?"

Stephan rubbed a hand along his nape. He didn't want to open up and share. He was a fool for loving her and a bigger fool for saying it out loud.

"Did you mean what you said just now?" Roselle's voice quivered.

He sighed. "Yes, I meant it."

"Why didn't you tell me before?"

"I guess I was scared too," he admitted.

She stepped between his legs and cupped his jaws. She brought her face so close to his, their noses brushed for a second. "I love you, too. I think I've loved you ever since Paris when I saw what a kind soul you are. That you're not shallow, but you're funny and thoughtful."

Stephan drew her thumb to his lips and kissed the tip. "Paris was definitely when you messed me up. From then on, I only had eyes for one woman. You. You've gotten a little fat around the middle, but I can work with it."

Roselle laughed through her tears.

"Maybe in another month or so we can see about getting rid of all *this*." He palmed her belly.

"I'll do my best."

He thumbed away her tears. "I missed you, babe."

"I missed you, too."

Using his forefinger, Stephan traced the curve of her bottom lip. His eyes tracked the motion, and his ears picked up her increased heavy breathing.

"I want you so much," Stephan whispered. "But I don't want to...is it okay if we...?"

Roselle nodded vigorously and locked her arms around his neck. "Yes, yes. It's fine." She seared her mouth to his and kissed him with all the longing and need that had accumulated over the months.

Stephan eased her arms from around his neck. "Hold up. Let's go upstairs. I want to make love to you properly."

She bit her bottom lip, and they both left the kitchen, hurrying up the stairs to Stephan's room.

CHAPTER 30

$\mathcal{L}$ying on his side behind Roselle, Stephan smoothed a hand over her belly, along one hip, and over her thigh, listening to her purr as he lovingly kissed her shoulders and back. He wanted to go slow, but she wasn't making it easy, what with her whimpering his name as he kissed her neck or gasping and arching her back when his hand squeezed the fullness of her breasts.

She seemed extra-sensitive, which was driving him crazy. He'd been horny for so long that before they started touching he'd been hard as granite and was sure he'd explode at any minute.

He inserted a finger between her legs, and she spread her thighs. Stephan lifted onto his elbow to watch her, eyes closed, lips parted, and a frown creasing her brows as she concentrated on what he was doing to her body. Stroking between her legs, he played with her engorged clit, and her curved spine arched further.

She circled her fabulous ass against his hard-on while his fingers continued to torment the swollen bundle of nerves between her legs.

She was getting close. Her hips moved with more urgency, and she reached back and grabbed the back of his head.

He dropped kisses on her neck. "My pussy is so wet. You want me to get in there?"

"Yes. Please," she whispered, looking at him through half-closed eyes.

She was so sexy like that. He kissed her cheek and ear. He kissed the corner of her mouth.

"Stephan," she moaned, the sound a mixture of desire and impatience.

"Okay, sweetness, I'll give you want you want," he said huskily.

He angled his hips toward her and slotted his body into hers. A wail of pleasure blew past her lips, and he almost came, listening to her while experiencing the softness of her bottom pressed into his pelvis.

She was his again, every inch of her body, and he savored this moment.

Slow, Stephan reminded himself. Which became extremely difficult when she reached back and sank her fingers into his ass cheeks, urging him deeper as she thrust her hips.

They moved together in slow motion, she throwing back her hips and he slicing into her wet body. Then Roselle moved with renewed vigor and panted heavily, striving toward release. Stephan joined her and increased the pace.

Finally, she came, quivering around him. Seconds later, he groaned out loud, gripping her hip and firing off two final pumps before he emptied inside her.

He groaned again and slumped on the bed, breathing heavily, and content for the first time in months.

CHAPTER 31

On his knees on the floor of the nursery, Stephan's gaze swept across all the parts of the crib spread out before him. They had gone to a doctor's appointment this morning, but he had taken the whole day off to spend time with Roselle. Now he wished he'd returned to work because of the daunting task of putting together the crib.

Roselle sat in an armchair, her head hidden behind an enormous, unfolded page of instructions. "According to this, we should start with part A and part B," she said.

"You know we can pay people to put together this furniture," Stephan said.

Roselle peered over the top of the sheet. "I heard you the first two times, but where's the fun in that?"

"Where's the fun in this?" he demanded.

"We don't need to have fun when we're doing it. Putting together the crib is an act of love for our baby."

"Or an act of torture for me because *we* are not putting together the crib. I am, which could take the rest of the day."

"Then *you* better get started." Roselle smiled sweetly.

Stephan glowered at her. "You're lucky I love you. I wouldn't put myself through this type of misery for just anybody." He took a deep breath. "Okay, let's do this."

He'd never put together a crib before, but if that's what she wanted, that's what he would do. He located parts A and B and set them aside together.

"Stephan."

"Yeah, babe." He piled all the screws and bolts together so they'd be easy to find.

When Roselle didn't respond, he glanced in her direction.

"Ask me again," she whispered. Her eyes held quiet longing.

"Ask you what?"

"Ask me to marry you." She spoke so softly, he barely heard her.

"I never asked you the first time."

Since they'd made love a few weeks ago, they'd become much closer. They shared his room now, and the only times he didn't fall asleep right away were when they stayed up late talking about the baby and their plans.

Looking into her face, he remembered how he'd screwed up when she first told him she was pregnant. This time he'd get it right, giving her the type of proposal she deserved, so she'd know how much she meant to him. How much he genuinely wanted her to be his wife, his partner in life.

Stephan came to his feet and walked over to where she sat on the chair. He lowered in front of her and set the instructions on the floor. Taking both of her hands in his, he looked into her eyes.

"Roselle, being with you, loving you, has affected me in so many ways. I'm a changed man because of you. I like who I am when I'm with you, and I like how you make me feel. I want to feel this way for the rest of my life. Would you do me the honor of becoming my wife?"

She'd pulled him out of a dark well of cynicism and reckless behavior, into the light. There was no one else he wanted to journey down life's road with but her.

"It would be an honor to become your wife. Yes!" Her face broke out into a huge grin.

They kissed briefly, their lips touching in a soft kiss.

Looking into her eyes, Stephan saw a bright future and wanted it to start sooner rather than later. "Let's get married right away before the baby comes. I'll leave work early on Friday, and we'll get our marriage license and get married this weekend, become husband and wife before the baby is born, the way I wanted in the first place."

"What about your family?"

"Getting married is about us. You, me, and our little girl. Unless you want a big wedding, say yes, and we'll become husband and wife in a few days."

"I don't care about a big wedding. I want to get married before she comes, too, so the answer is yes!" Roselle squealed.

He enveloped her in a big hug and rested his forehead against hers.

"We're doing this," she whispered.

"We're doing this," he confirmed.

They kissed again, leisurely, enjoying each other and the emotional moment now that they'd committed to spending their lives together.

Stephan rose from his kneeling position and walked to where the parts of the crib were spread out. He stood over the pieces.

"Okay, I separated A and B. What's next?"

Roselle let out a pained sound, and he immediately swung in her direction.

"What's the matter?"

She rubbed the top of her belly and groaned, biting down on her bottom lip. "I don't know... I wonder if I'm having contractions, but that can't be right. We still have a few weeks left. The baby can't be coming now. She's too early."

"When did you start having contractions?" Stephan asked.

Shifting in the chair, Roselle exhaled through her mouth and rubbed her lower back. "After we left the doctor's office."

"And you didn't say anything!" Stephan exclaimed.

"Don't yell at me! I thought they might be the Braxton Hicks contractions again. Except these are stronger, and they're coming closer together now." Her eyes filled with worry.

"I'm calling the doctor."

Turning in a circle, Stephan frantically searched the room, trying to tamp down his panic because he didn't want to alarm Roselle. His phone was on the window sill, and he rushed over and picked it up. He dialed Dr. Tambo's number, and while the phone rang, he knelt beside Roselle's chair and took her hand. Her hand was shaking, and he gave her a reassuring squeeze.

When the doctor answered, he put her on speaker and explained that Roselle was having contractions.

"How far apart are they?" the doctor asked.

Roselle answered in a small voice. "Um, I'd say ten to twelve minutes apart, but this last one was almost twenty. Should we be worried?"

"Everything looked fine when I examined you this morning, so for now I'm not worried. Don't be alarmed." The doctor's voice was warm and reassuring. "This is your body preparing you to deliver your baby girl. Here's what I want you to do. If you haven't already, write down the times between the contractions, and if they get to five minutes apart and last for about an hour, call me. Definitely call me if your water breaks, you experience any bleeding, or if something feels off, okay?"

"Okay," Roselle said.

"Do you have any more questions or concerns?"

"No, that's it," Roselle replied.

"Call me if you need me."

"Thanks, Dr. Tambo." Stephan hung up the phone.

He and Roselle looked at each other, and he figured the same thought was going through her head as was going through his.

"I can't have this baby right now. We still have a million things to do. The crib isn't ready, and we have to get married first."

He set the phone on the floor and clasped her hand in both of his. "Babe, forget about the crib. I can hire someone to put it together for us. As for getting married first, that's not going to happen if the baby is coming."

"I want to be your wife when I have this baby!"

Stephan kept his voice calm. "If you're going into labor, that's impossible."

"Dr. Tambo said we still have time, and who knows, this could be another false alarm. Let's get married today. Let's not wait."

"Sweetness, we can't get married today."

"We have to. I'm not having this baby. I want to be your wife first."

"You don't get a lot of say in the matter. Babies come when they're supposed to."

"You think I don't know that!" Roselle yelled. "We need a marriage license and someone to marry us before I deliver. You're rich. Figure it out." Tears welled in her eyes.

"Okay, calm down. Can I say one thing, though? We could have been married months ago."

"Really, Stephan? You're saying I told you so right now? You said yourself you didn't exactly ask me to marry you before. You basically told me that your mother would force you to marry me. So excuse me if I didn't jump at the chance!"

She was so cute when she was mad. He grabbed her face and pressed a hard kiss to her lips. Then he pulled back and grinned. "You want to be my wife today? Then, damn it, I'm going to make it happen."

He picked up his phone and jumped up. First, he put in a call to the concierge service he used and gave them the task of tracking down an officiant and getting a car and driver to his house. He wanted to be prepared to go to the hospital if she indeed was in labor.

Next, he went in search of one of Brit Wong's cards. Usually, if he was in trouble, he called Sylvie and she called Brit, but Stephan had received cards from the attorney before. After a search that took longer than he liked, he found one in a drawer in a table a few feet from his bed.

Marching back to the nursery, he dialed the attorney's direct line. Brit answered right away, and Stephan explained the situation —that Roselle was in labor and he needed a marriage license so they could be married today.

"Both you and Roselle have to be present to obtain the license," Brit explained.

Stephan kept his gaze on Roselle. One hand rested on her belly, and she shifted in the chair as if trying to get comfortable.

"That's not going to happen, so you'll have to do it without us being there," Stephan said, pacing the floor.

"And how do you propose I do that?"

"I'm sure you'll think of something."

"I'm not a magician, Stephan," Brit said dryly.

"Make it happen, Brit. You've worked magic before. If you can get me out of jail in the middle of the night on a weekend, you can get me a marriage license today before my fiancée has our baby. I'm counting on you."

There was a pause. Then Brit chuckled. "All right, send me a copy of her driver's license. I already have your information. I'll do my best."

"Thanks!"

Hanging up, Stephan became confident he and Roselle would be married before the end of the day, and hopefully before their little bundle made an appearance. That was, until Roselle cried out and her face crumpled in pain.

He rushed to her side. "Babe, do you need anything? Talk to me."

Roselle breathed heavily through her mouth for at least thirty seconds before she answered. Tears filled her eyes. "Seems our baby has other ideas about us getting married before she gets here. The contractions are coming closer together. How did the calls go?" She winced, holding her round belly.

"Good. Attorney Wong is working on getting the marriage

license. No guarantees, but I need a copy of your ID to pull it off. The concierge service will have a car sent and find us a minister to perform the ceremony. But babe, what do you mean the contractions are coming closer together? Do we need to call the doctor?"

Roselle averted her eyes to a window in the room.

Taking her chin, Stephan twisted her head around to face him. "Do I need to call the doctor? How far apart are the contractions?"

She bit down on her bottom lip. "Six minutes."

"Shit." His heart thumped erratically in his chest. His mother complained she'd been in labor with him for twenty hours, but his kid was racing to come out.

Roselle grabbed his arm. "We still have time. Dr. Tambo said we should call when the contractions are five minutes apart."

Stephan had his doubts, but now that they'd made the decision to get married, he wanted her to be his wife before their baby was born, too. He placed his hands over her belly. "Hang in there, baby. We need you to stay put a little longer."

Roselle nodded and placed her hands over his. "Hang in there a little bit longer, sweetie."

Forty-five minutes later, a photo of Roselle's ID had been texted to Attorney Wong, and a driver had arrived and waited in an SUV in the driveway.

Roselle let out another wail of pain, and Stephan checked the time. He entered the information into the Notes app of his phone and saw a disturbing pattern. The contractions were coming much faster now.

"I'm calling Dr. Tambo."

Roselle didn't protest, she was too busy breathing through her mouth, eyes closed, head resting against the back of the chair.

Stephan dialed the number and paced the floor, running a hand over the back of his head. "Hello, Dr. Tambo? For the past thirty minutes, the contractions are only four minutes apart now. Should we—"

"Get her to the hospital. I'll meet you there."

Stephan froze as fear gripped him. He ended the call. "We gotta go. Dr. Tambo's on her way to the hospital."

Tears filled Roselle's eyes.

He walked over to where she sat and dropped to his haunches. "We weren't planning to get married until I asked you to marry me today. And it's clearly not going to happen until after the baby is born. We need to get to the hospital right now, or you'll probably have our baby on this chair. There's nobody else here but you and me, and I don't know the first thing about delivering a baby. I want the two of you to be safe. Don't you want the two of you to be safe?"

She blinked rapidly, obviously distressed. "Yes," she said, voice trembling.

"Then let's do this. Come on." Stephan helped her up, and they carefully made their way down the staircase. When they almost reached the bottom, the doorbell rang. They looked at each other.

"Maybe it's the minister?" she whispered.

Another contraction tore through her body and she cried out, doubling over, gripping the railing.

"One minute!" Stephan yelled at the door.

He held onto Roselle and rubbed her back until the pain passed.

"Go," she panted, hugging the railing.

Stephan hurried to the door and swung it open. As luck would have it, both the minister and Attorney Wong had arrived at the same time.

Brit held up the marriage license. "I have it."

The minister, an older male wearing glasses and his entire head gray, stuck out a hand. "Pastor Hunting. I hear you're getting married today."

Stephan quickly shook his hand and ushered them inside. "Yeah, we are. Come on, let's do this fast. My fiancée's in labor."

Walking swiftly, they went to the staircase, and Roselle stood there, eyes wide. She looked terrified.

"My water just broke."

CHAPTER 32

"That's it. I'm getting you out of here. We don't have time to get married," Stephan said grimly. He scooped her up in his arms.

"I can marry you in the car," Pastor Hunting quickly said. "We can right this wrong in God's eyes."

Stephan opened his mouth to let the officiant know where he could shove his judgmental comment, but since he really wanted to marry Roselle and needed the pastor to do it, he swallowed his sharp rebuke.

"Yes! Let's do that," Roselle said. She let out a pained cry and clung to Stephan, burying her face in his shoulder.

"I've got you," he whispered reassuringly.

Their party of four rushed out of the house and Stephan settled Roselle in the back seat of the SUV and climbed in after her. When Pastor Hunting jumped in the front, Stephan tapped the back of the driver's seat. "Get us to the hospital as fast as you can."

"Will do."

The driver pulled off the estate, racing down the street with Stephan cradling Roselle in the rear, and Brit following in his black Mercedes.

Pastor Hunting turned to face them in the back seat and started. "We are gathered here today, to unite this man—"

"Skip that part and talk faster," Stephan urged.

"Okay." Pastor Hunting cleared his throat. "Do you, Stephan Brooks, take this woman to be your lawfully wedded wife? To have and to hold, in sickness and in health, in good times and bad, for richer or poorer, keeping solely unto her for as long as you both shall live?"

He gazed at Roselle, who was breathing heavily and cradling her belly with both arms.

"I do." He'd never been more certain of anything in his life. He kissed the top of her head.

The driver swung a hard left, and Stephan braced a hand against the ceiling of the car.

"Do you, Roselle Parker—"

Roselle let out a scream of agony and grabbed the driver's seat. The driver glanced back at her with concern. His gaze met Stephan's in the rearview mirror before returning to the road.

"Breathe, babe, breathe," Stephan said, rubbing her back.

She couldn't talk for long seconds because of the excruciating pain. Panting, she collapsed against the seat. "I am breathing!"

Pastor Hunting nervously wiped his brow. "Do you, Roselle Parker, take this man to be your lawfully wedded husband? To have and to hold, in sickness and in health, in good times and bad, for richer or poorer, keeping solely unto him for as long as you both shall live?"

He'd barely finished the question when Roselle belted out, "I do!"

"Is there a ring?" the officiant asked.

"No," Stephan answered.

"By the authority vested in me by the state of Georgia, I now pronounce you husband and wife. What God hath joined together, let no man or woman put asunder. You may kiss... er... congratulations."

Stephan held Roselle's hand and rested his head against hers. "We're almost there, babe."

"We're married. We did it." A happy tear trickled down one of her cheeks.

He wiped away the tear and grinned down at his bride. Man, she was beautiful. How did he get so lucky?

The driver pulled to a hard stop in front of the hospital doors.

Stephan hopped out and ran up to the reception desk. "My wife's in labor," he announced.

A Black nurse immediately jumped up, but he didn't wait around. He rushed back out to help Roselle out of the car.

Brit pulled in directly behind them and hopped out of his Mercedes. "You need to sign this," he said, waving the license.

Roselle took several deep breaths through her mouth, gritted her teeth, and signed her name. Stephan did the same.

The nurse came rushing out with a wheelchair. "We need to get her up to the maternity floor."

Roselle sank onto the chair, and the nurse wheeled her in.

Beaming, Pastor Hunting held up the license. "I'll take care of this. Congratulations!"

"Congratulations!" Brit said.

"Thank you!" Stephan went after Roselle and the nurse.

Roselle let out a scream, tossing back her head and cradling her belly. Beads of sweat dotted right below the hairline on her forehead.

Seeing her suffer and unable to do anything about it made Stephan feel helpless. "Should she get something for the pain?"

"The doctor will decide that. Let's get her upstairs first, okay?" The nurse looked at him with sympathetic eyes. She'd probably seen plenty of men lose their minds because they couldn't alleviate their partner's pain.

They rode the elevator to the maternity floor, and when the doors opened, Dr. Tambo, a tall African woman with dark brown skin and round cheeks, was waiting for them.

She smiled encouragingly. "How are we doing?" she asked in a soothing voice.

"Awful," Roselle whimpered.

"Contractions are only three minutes apart now and her water broke," Stephan added.

"That's good news! That means your little girl is on her way." The doctor signaled to one of the nurses on the maternity floor. "Let's get her into the delivery room and changed."

Stephan was about to follow, but a white nurse came out of nowhere and placed a hand on his arm. "Before you go, I need to get you registered."

"I need to be with her."

"You will be shortly, but we need to confirm a few things. It'll only take a few minutes. Name?"

"Stephan Brooks and Roselle Parker," he said irritably, his eyes following Roselle as she disappeared down the hall.

The registration did not only take a few minutes. He contemplated leaving the nurse with her stupid paperwork, but he answered all the questions though he desperately wanted to be in the delivery room with Roselle, to give her his support.

Once he finished with the formalities and signed a few papers, the nurse escorted him to the delivery room. "You'll want to change out of these clothes or protect them." She opened the door and handed him some scrubs.

He couldn't see Roselle because a curtain was pulled around the bed she was lying on, but he heard her moans, the voices of the medical staff, and machines beeping.

"You can change in there." The nurse pointed to the restroom.

"Give me another big push," he heard Dr. Tambo say. Roselle's high-pitched scream lasted for a long time. He threw on the scrubs and booties on his feet and quickly exited the bathroom.

He heard Roselle sobbing. "Where's my husband? Where's Stephan? I can't do this without him. Please, where is he?" Panic had crept to the edges of her voice.

Husband. He was her husband. She was his wife.

"I'm right here," he said in a loud voice. He stepped around the curtain to see Dr. Tambo positioned between Roselle's legs, and two nurses standing close by.

Roselle stretched out a hand and he took it, squeezing gently.

He kissed her knuckles. "Where'd you think I was? Did you think I'd left you?"

She rubbed away the tears that trickled down the corners of her eyes.

"I don't know. I panicked," she whispered, eyes wet.

He brushed damp, stray hairs away from her forehead. "You're not alone anymore, remember? I'll always be right here, okay?"

She nodded and visibly relaxed against the pillows. Then another contraction hit.

"Push," Dr. Tambo said.

Roselle rose up off the bed and yelled, voice hoarse, eyes squinting as she gripped the mattress. When the moment passed, she fell back, sucking air into her lungs with heavy inhalations. "I can't... I can't do this. It's too hard."

Stephan kissed her forehead, wishing he could take her pain away. He gently stroked her hair. "You're doing great, babe. Our little girl is almost here."

Seconds later, Roselle lifted her upper body into a tense crunch as she yelled. She crushed Stephan's forearm in a death hold, and he gritted his teeth against her tight grip. Panting heavily, she fell back against the pillows again, looking exhausted.

"That's it. I see the head. We're almost there. Give me another big push," Dr. Tambo coaxed.

Roselle pushed hard again, her entire body shaking with the stress and strain of the delivery. Stephan whispered soothing words, giving the support she needed as her fingernails sank into his flesh.

Her hoarse cries filled the delivery room and were finally joined by the wail of their little girl.

CHAPTER 33

*R*oselle came awake slowly. She shifted in the bed and moaned, freezing when her sore, aching body reminded her she'd given birth hours before.

"Careful," a voice warned from off to her right.

She shifted again, wincing as she twisted her head to see Sylvie Johnson seated on a chair beside the bed. What was she doing here?

She must have come straight from work. She wore her long hair secured at the nape, and a burgundy peplum dress with long sleeves ruffled around the wrists. Very little jewelry. Stylish and elegant as always.

"How are you feeling?" the older woman asked.

"Fine." Roselle glanced around the private suite. They were alone. She wondered what Stephan's mother would say. She probably wouldn't be pleased about the rushed marriage. She braced herself.

"You can't possibly be feeling fine. You pushed another human being out of your body."

Roselle smiled weakly. "I feel like I've been run over by a car," she admitted.

"That's about right. But your little one is worth it." Sylvie stood and went over to a table. She poured ice water from a pitcher into a glass and handed it to Roselle.

"Thank you." She swallowed the water gratefully. When she'd drained the glass, Sylvie took it.

"More?"

"No, that's enough."

Sylvie replaced it on the table and remained standing next to the bed.

"I had them increase the temperature in the room. It was freezing cold, and I made it clear that my daughter-in-law needed to be comfortable, not freezing to death. Are you comfortable?"

"Yes." Sylvie had referred to her as her daughter-in-law!

"Stephan explained to me that you were married en route to the hospital. I'm happy that you're both married. That's what I wanted in the first place. I'm disappointed in the way that it happened. Of course you know, we will have a proper celebration, once you're feeling better?"

"Yes," Roselle said, because that was the right answer.

"Good. We'll discuss the particulars at a later date. Stephan stepped out for a few minutes. He's been here the entire time, watching over you and Avery." Her face softened when she said her granddaughter's name. "He's going to be a great father. I don't know if you've seen him with his nieces, but they adore him. You won't be lacking in support. Take advantage and get as much rest as possible. You're going to need it with a newborn."

Roselle nodded her understanding, still waiting for the fireworks or whatever was coming. She didn't know what was coming, but she sensed there was more Sylvie wanted to say, and a coil of tension kept her from completely relaxing in her presence.

"I hope you know I expect you back at work after your maternity leave."

"You want me back?"

Sylvie had been cordial during the pregnancy, but Roselle assumed her kindness had been because of Stephan and the new grandbaby on the way. After having an affair with her son, the abrupt way she'd quit the company, and the rushed wedding, Roselle had been certain Sylvie wouldn't want her back at the company. She'd been prepared to find another position somewhere else when she started looking again.

"But of course I want you back. You were a great fashion director. You're good at your job, you have a great eye, and I trust your judgment."

"But what will people think?"

"About what?"

"About you hiring me back now that I'm married to your son."

Sylvie pursed her lips. "I will let you in on a little secret. I don't care what people think, and neither should you. Try it. Practice it. It gets easier over time. If I worried about what people think, I wouldn't be as successful as I am. Frankly, people can say whatever they want. Who would dare say it to your face? Live your life the way you desire—the way you *deserve*. Let the busybodies live theirs being miserable. They are not your problem."

It would take time for her to get to the point where she completely ignored other people's opinions of her, but just the idea of having that much freedom gave her a sense of relief, as if a lead yoke had been lifted from around her neck.

"Now, one more thing," Sylvie said.

Roselle tensed. *Here it comes.*

"Stephan told me something terrible happened to you when you were a teenager. I won't bring it up again. I will leave it up to you to do that, but I want you to know that I'm aware. And I want you to understand something." She leaned over the bed, and her light brown eyes—so much like Stephan's—were open and kind but contained a fierce light. So different from what she'd expected to see. "Listen to me very carefully. You are not alone. We do not turn our back on family, and now you have a whole family of people who care about you, on two sides. Brooks on my husband's side and Johnsons on my side. But more importantly, anyone who dares to hurt you again will have to deal with me. And let me assure you, my darling, no one wants to deal with me. Are we clear?"

"Yes."

"Good." Sylvie tucked the sheets more snugly around her.

Stephan stepped into the room and paused in the doorway. "Mother?" Worry filled his voice.

"Hello, darling. I'm having a little chat with Roselle. I'll be off now and leave you two alone. Roselle, remember what I said." Sylvie folded her coat over one arm. She strode to the door and stopped in front of Stephan. She tapped her cheek, and he kissed it. "Keep me updated on Avery's progress. I'll stop by in a few days to see her. Have a good night. Roselle, get some rest."

"Yes, ma'am."

Sylvie turned a sharp eye on her son. "Make sure she gets some rest."

"I will."

When she'd left, Stephan rushed over to the bed. "I was gone for five minutes. Five goddamn minutes. What did she say to you?" He set a cup of coffee on the table beside the bed.

Tears filled Roselle's eyes.

Stephan cursed. "I'll have a talk with her. I can't believe she'd come at you while you're lying in a hospital bed."

"She didn't. It's okay." She sniffed.

"She must have said something. You're about to cry. What did she say?"

Roselle laughed through her tears. "She welcomed me into the family."

The angry frown disappeared from his face, and he eased onto the edge of the bed to keep from jostling her. He took her hand. "She's right. You're part of the family now, with everything that means. The good and the bad."

"Mostly good."

"Don't be too sure," Stephan said dryly.

She grinned, knowing he was half-joking. He loved his family, no matter how much he liked to complain about them.

She squeezed his hand in hers. "We did it," she said.

"You did it."

"*We*. You were with me all the way. With you beside me, I felt like nothing could go wrong." A tear slipped from the corner of her eye.

"Hey." He frowned and brushed it away with his thumb.

"I'm okay. I'm happy, that's all."

He kissed her forehead and the corner of her eye.

"I love you," Roselle said. It felt so good to say it now. She could say the words whenever and as often as she wanted.

A playful smile graced his handsome features. "Not as much as I love you."

EPILOGUE

$\mathcal{T}$he wedding reception for Malik Brooks and Lindsay Winthrop was winding down at The Winthrop Hotel in downtown Atlanta. The wedding band played a low tempo beat, while their lead singer, a lovely Black woman wearing giant hoop earrings, belted out lyrics in a husky voice that should have been selling out arenas instead of providing entertainment to a much smaller crowd in the ballroom of a hotel.

Malik and Lindsay slow-danced with other couples around them doing the same. Lindsay wore an haute-couture off-the-shoulder gown, and her short hair brushed back from her face and flipped up at the ends using extensions. Their love was evident in the way their eyes locked on each other as if there was no one else around.

Stephan's eyes scoured the room and once again landed on Reese and Nina huddled together in a corner. He was pretty sure Nina hadn't had a chance to talk to too many people since Reese had barely left her side the entire night.

Roselle sidled up to him with a drink in hand and looped an arm around his waist. "Who's the girl Reese has been talking to all night?"

"That's Nina, Lindsay's younger sister."

"Does she and Reese have a thing going?"

"No." He had a bad feeling that Nina was going to break his brother's heart. "She's the one who got away."

"Oh."

"You ready to go?"

"Yes."

Stephan took her hand, and they said their goodbyes on the way out. When they arrived at home, the sitter told them that she fed Avery a few minutes before and she was still awake. After they changed into comfortable clothes, they went into the nursery.

"Hi, sweetie," Roselle cooed.

She was rewarded with a toothless smile.

Avery and Roselle had spent an extra day in the hospital before the doctor gave the go-ahead for their release, and as new parents, she and Stephan had hovered and watched over their daughter with the tenacity of lions. Stephan had taken off a month from work. This week Roselle started doing occasional work-related tasks from home because she missed her job, but she wouldn't be back at SJ Brands full-time for another three months.

"Are we watching a movie tonight?" Stephan asked.

"Yes." Roselle lifted the baby from the crib.

"Which one?" They exited the room and made their way down-stairs toward the theater room.

"*Black Panther.*"

"Oh, right, because somebody hasn't seen it yet."

"I wanted to, but I never got around to seeing it."

"I'm seriously thinking about taking away your black card."

"Please don't," Roselle said with mock distress.

Instead of sitting in the high-backed chairs, they settled next to each other at the rear of the room on a comfy sofa that reclined.

"I won't if you give me a kiss."

"I can handle that."

Their lips came together in a quick, soft kiss. Her lips were so sweet. He'd never tire of them.

"Do I get to keep my black card now?" Roselle asked with exaggerated hopefulness.

Stephan licked his lips. "For now. Consider yourself on probation."

"Is there anything I can do to change that?"

He leaned over and whispered in her ear, "Meet me where the magic happens and we'll see."

Roselle giggled. "You're awful."

"Yet you still married me."

"Best decision I ever made."

She puckered her lips and gave him another quick smooch.

Roselle liked to lean on him when they watched movies, so Stephan took the baby, whose heavy-lidded eyes signaled she'd be fast asleep very soon.

Roselle curled up her feet and rested her head on his shoulder, and Stephan scrolled through the movie options until he arrived at *Black Panther*. He chose it, and the opening credits appeared.

"Don't fall asleep," he warned, looping an arm around her shoulders.

"I won't." Roselle smothered a yawn with her palm.

She'd be asleep in fifteen minutes, max.

With his daughter dozing on his chest, and his wife about to fall asleep at his side, Stephan smiled to himself, thinking about how much his life had changed in the past year.

He was truly living the good life now.

More Brooks Family

Check out the other books in the Brooks Family series and get to know the other family members!

Find out how Simone Brooks met and fell in love with nightclub owner Cameron Bennett in A Passionate Love.

Read how Oscar Brooks and Sylvie Johnson found their way back together after fifteen years apart in Passion Rekindled.

Read how Ella Brooks finds love in an unexpected place, the second time around with Detective Tyrone Evers in Do Over.

Experience the fireworks between Malik Brooks and relationship expert Lindsay Winthrop when they enter into a fake relationship in Wild Thoughts.

Find out why Stephan Brooks will risk it all for fashion director Roselle Parker in Two Nights in Paris.

ALSO BY DELANEY DIAMOND

Brooks Family series

- A Passionate Love
- Passion Rekindled
- Do Over
- Wild Thoughts
- Two Nights in Paris

Johnson Family series

- Unforgettable
- Perfect
- Just Friends
- The Rules
- Good Behavior

Royal Brides

- Princess of Zamibia
- Princess of Estoria

Love Unexpected series

- The Blind Date
- The Wrong Man
- An Unexpected Attraction
- The Right Time
- One of the Guys
- That Time in Venice

Latin Men series

- The Arrangement
- Fight for Love
- Private Acts
- The Ultimate Merger
- Second Chances
- More Than a Mistress
- Undeniable
- Hot Latin Men: Vol. I (print anthology)
- Hot Latin Men: Vol. II (print anthology)

Hawthorne Family series

- The Temptation of a Good Man
- A Hard Man to Love
- Here Comes Trouble
- For Better or Worse
- Hawthorne Family Series: Vol. I (print anthology)
- Hawthorne Family Series: Vol. II (print anthology)

Bailar series (sweet/clean romance)

- Worth Waiting For

Stand Alones

- Still in Love
- Subordinate Position
- Heartbreak in Rio

Other

- Audiobooks
- Free Stories

ABOUT THE AUTHOR

Delaney Diamond is the USA Today Bestselling Author of sweet, sensual, passionate romance novels. Originally from the U.S. Virgin Islands, she now lives in Atlanta, Georgia. She reads romance novels, mysteries, thrillers, and a fair amount of nonfiction. When she's not busy reading or writing, she's in the kitchen trying out new recipes, dining at one of her favorite restaurants, or traveling to an interesting locale.

Enjoy free reads and the first chapter of all her novels on her website. Join her mailing list to get sneak peeks, notices of sale prices, and find out about new releases.

Join her mailing list
www.delaneydiamond.com

f facebook.com/DelaneyDiamond

twitter.com/DelaneyDiamond

pinterest.com/DelaneyDiamond

instagram.com/authordelaneydiamond

CPSIA information can be obtained
at www.ICGtesting.com
Printed in the USA
LVHW081327280619
622657LV00030B/403/P